Dark Angels

Dark Angels

Lesbian Vampire Stories

Edited by

PAM KEESEY

Published in the United States by Cleis Press Inc.,
P.O. Box 8933, Pittsburgh, Pennsylvania 15221, and
P.O. Box 14684, San Francisco, California 94114.

Book design and production: Pete Ivey
Cover photograph: Phyllis Christopher
Cleis logo art: Juana Alicia

First Edition.
Printed in the United States.
10 9 8 7 6 5 4 3 2

"Wanting" by Amelia G first appeared in *Blue Blood* #4 (1994). Reprinted with permission. "Blood Wedding" by Gary Bowen was originally published in *Vampire Dreams* (Obelesk Books, Elkton, MD, 1993). Reprinted by permission of the author. "Cinnamon Roses" by Renee M. Charles first appeared in *Blood Kiss* (Circlet Press, Boston, MA, 1994). Reprinted by permission of the author. "The Bloody Countess" by Alejandra Pizarnik is from *Other Fires: Short Fiction by Latin American Women* edited by Alberto Manguel (1986). Reprinted by permission of Crown Publishers, Inc. "The Countess Visonti" is excerpted from *Sardia: A Story of Love* by Cora Linn Daniels (Lee and Shepard Pub, Boston, MA, 1891).

Special thanks to Peter Larsen of Dreamhaven Books in Minneapolis who has been a goldmine of vampire literature, magazines, and assorted other vampire paraphanalia.

Library of Congress Cataloging-in-Publication Data

Dark angels : Lesbian vampire stories / edited by Pam Keesey.
p. cm.
Includes bibliographical references.
ISBN 1-57344-014-0 (paper). — ISBN 1-57344-015-9 (cloth)
1. Lesbian vampires—Fiction. 2. Lesbians' writings, American.
3. Horror tales, American. 4. Lesbians—Fiction. I. Keesey, Pam.
1964–
PS648.V35D37 1995
813'.0108375—dc20 95-34776
CIP

Contents

Contents

To Janne

and

To my parents

who have been more supportive than they'll ever know.

Introduction

PAM KEESEY

THIS HAS BEEN a remarkable two years for me. I've been both delighted and astounded by the response to *Daughters of Darkness: Lesbian Vampire Stories* (Cleis Press, 1993), my first collection. What I thought might be a dust-covered tome buried deep in the library stacks has been passionately received by not only hard-core vampire fans but by an amazingly diverse group of readers. *Daughters of Darkness* has been read by vampire fans who have never read lesbian fiction, lesbians who have never read vampire fiction, and all sorts of people who found the cover just too compelling to pass up! Even my parents now consider my childhood obsession a legitimate endeavor.

I've always been a vampire fan, the quintessential closet collector of vampire lore and literature, squirreling away vampire fact and fiction whenever it came my way. Friends read trashy romances, mysteries, detective novels, but for me, it was always vampire stories. The thought that I would make my private obsession public was far removed—until one afternoon shortly after the release of Francis Ford Coppola's film *Dracula*. Along with all the marketing tie-ins came a flood of vampire anthologies. I would scan their tables of contents for Pat Califia's "The Vampire" or Katherine Forrest's "Oh Captain, My Captain" or some other story that featured lesbians and/or lesbian imagery. The only story that showed up with any regularity was "Carmilla"—a classic by anyone's standards. I knew that I couldn't be the only lesbian who loved vampires and so, *Daughters of Darkness* was, if you'll pardon the expression, brought to light.

Dark Angels is not the sequel to *Daughters of Darkness*, although it was born of the same love of vampire lore and lesbian imagery. *Daughters of Darkness* and *Dark Angels* are like siblings—the family resemblance is there, but each has its own identity, its own personality. *Daughters of Darkness* is a collection of lesbian fiction featuring vampires and vampire-related themes. They are stories of lesbian romance, of coming out, of lesbians alone and lesbians in community. It is a collection of stories deeply rooted in the women's movement and lesbian and gay civil rights. *Dark Angels*, on the other hand, is a collection of vampire stories featuring lesbians and lesbian-related themes. They are stories of grief and hope, of life and death, of spirit and body. They are stories of darkness and of blood, both as substance and as symbol.

Vampires, more than any other supernatural creature, have been defined by their association with blood. Vampires are most often thought of as revenants—those who come back from the dead—and therefore need the blood of the living to maintain their undead state. In older vampire lore, the moon also held a particular power in investing the dead with life. Governing the cycles of women's blood, it was the source of all life and the resting place for those who had yet to be born. When it was time, the moon gave forth the spirit and soul of the child who would be born of a particular mother's womb.

As the vampire is a nocturnal creature, it follows that the vampire would have a special relationship to the moon. This relationship played an important role in the vampire literature of the nineteenth century. In John Polidori's "The Vampyre," Lord Ruthven had instructed his henchmen that in the event of his death, they should take him to the pinnacle of a nearby hill so that his body could be exposed to "the first cold ray of the moon that rose after his death." When Lord Ruthven is killed, the moon's rays revive him, and he is free to carry on his bloody rampage. Bram Stoker broke with the tradition of the vampire being governed by the stages of the moon, using it instead as an atmospheric device. Since then, the moon has been primarily associated with werewolves. The magic of the blood, however, carries on.

The blood in vampire lore is usually taken from the neck, the wrist or the crook of the arm. If menstrual blood is even mentioned, it is rarely the central element in any vampire story. Only in the last thirty years or so, largely a result of the women's movement, has menstruation become a topic for casual conversation. The roles of goddess mythology and the accompanying lore of menstrual blood and lunar cycles in the development of the vampire legends we now take so readily for granted are still, for the most part, invisible and unknown.

Blood, of course, is the very essence of life. Along with water and oxygen, it is one of the most important fluids that make life on this planet possible. Blood has always had an important symbolic power. In ancient times, blood offerings implored protection, purification and salvation. Blood was, and is, a covenant. In some cultures, to be "blood brothers/blood sisters" was as important as having the same kin; the same marriage and child-bearing restrictions applied. Blood was an essential element in ancient necromancy, whether symbolic or real, and is still found in many ritual practices throughout the world. In taking Holy Communion, the recipient is accepting "the flesh of my flesh, the blood of my blood" in holy sacrament with Jesus Christ.

Menstrual blood, at one time called "the liquor of life," was considered to be the most powerful blood of all. The magic of creation was thought to rest in menstrual blood, which women gave forth in harmony with the cycles of the moon. The blood was sometimes retained in the womb to "coagulate" into a baby. The power of menstrual blood, whether for good or ill, is found over and over again in the religion, mythology and folklore of peoples around the world.

The belief that the dead crave blood in order to live is deeply imbedded in the belief in the magical properties of blood. Menstrual blood, also known as lunar blood, was considered to be especially powerful because it gave life, not only by coursing through the veins of the living, but also through the miracle of birth. Many believed that blood contained the life-essence: the soul. That women could shed blood without injury contributed to its mysterious and sacred essence.

The roots of the vampire can be found in early images of the Goddess. The Goddess and the vampire share two very important symbols: blood, and the moon. Vampires, like the Goddess, are associated with life, death and rebirth. Vampires are also associated with blood and death, also realms of the Goddess. The Goddess was the primordial being who created the universe and all the laws governing it. She was the ruler of all nature, including fate, time, eternity, truth, wisdom, life and death. She was honored in her three aspects: the young woman, the life-giving mother and the aging wisewoman. Through the early centuries of recorded history, the image of the Goddess was broken down into innumerable "goddesses," using different titles or names and emphasizing particular realms or features. The Goddess as young woman was a virgin; the Goddess in her middle-age was a mother; the Goddess as elderly woman was the death-giver or the devouring mother.

It is in the image of the devouring mother that it is easiest to see the bloodthirsty Goddess as vampire. Kali, a Hindu deity, is probably one of the most well-known of the devouring goddesses. Kali is the dark aspect of the Mother-Goddess Devi. She is said to have fangs or tusks, four arms, claws wielding swords and spears, and a necklace of severed heads. In one story, she joins the goddess Durga to fight the demon Raktabija, whom she defeats by drinking all of his blood. Kali is also a prominent deity within Tantric Hinduism as Creator, Protector and Destroyer. In Tantra, the way of salvation is through the sensual delights of this world. Kali represents those forbidden pleasures and teaches that life relies on death, and in confronting death, there is liberation.

In the image of the Goddess as vampire, the sexual aspect of the Goddess has been demonized. The Goddess has become the vamp—a woman who destroys men using her sexuality. She is the temptress who brings death and destruction in her wake. Yet there are still traces of the divine image of the Goddess. Isis, Milton tells us, was a fallen angel. Lilith, too, was a fallen angel—the Cabalistic sect identified Lilith as one of God's top ten angels. Although the current iconography would have us believe that angels are sexless beings, much like the cherubs that are currently so popular, the early angels, like the early goddesses, were sexual beings. Dark angels, like the dark goddesses, desired sexual union, and it was the failure to deny their sexual needs that led them astray.

Lilith, a relic of the Babylonian myth of Lilitu, is a Jewish demoness said to be the first wife of Adam. Legend has it that she refused to succumb to Adam's authority, flying away to the Red Sea—the dwelling place of demons—rather than "lying" beneath him. There she lived in a cave, taking the demons who lived there as her lovers and from those unions, gave birth to a great multitude of demons. God sent three angels—Senoy, Sansenoy and Semangeloff—after Lilith to command her to return to Adam. She refused, even after the angels threatened to kill one hundred of her children every day (apparently there were many more demon children who would survive in order to bring woe and grief to all humankind). In retaliation, she swore her vengeance on newborn infants. She said that she could be stopped from snatching the souls of babes only if confronted by an amulet bearing the names of the three angels. The amulets became a regular feature of Jewish life and are still used in some Orthodox Jewish circles.

Lilith's sins did not stop there. She would also slip into the beds of men, seducing them in their sleep, causing sinful dreams and nocturnal emissions. From those unions, Lilith bore even more demon children who continued to populate the earth. Lilith is a recurring figure in Jewish tales of the supernatural, and her resemblance to the vampire is strong. She is said to dwell in darkness, with dark hair and eyes and luminescent skin. She has the ability to change herself into any form she wishes, human or animal, and can appear as an old hag or a young, beautiful woman. She steals life energy, from children in the form of their souls and from men in the form of their "seed" or "life essence." She seduces women from goodness and turns them to lust and vanity. She is the namesake of many vampire women, some of the more recent and well-known being the Marvel comic book character "Lilith, Daughter of Dracula," the film, *The Mark of Lilith*, and Robbi Sommer's "Lilith" (see *Daughters of Darkness*). Lilith is known by many names, including the Queen of Sheba, Lilidtha, Agrath, but perhaps most interesting is that one of her recurring alternative names is Kali.

Like Lilith, the Greek *lamiai* are a class of female demons who can transform themselves, usually into the form of beautiful women, in order to attract and seduce men. The *lamiai* take their name from Lamia, who is said to have been a Libyan queen. Lamia was loved by the king of the Greek gods, Zeus. Hera, Zeus' wife, murdered Lamia's children in a jealous rage. Consumed by grief and vengeance, Lamia became a demon who devoured children or sucked their blood. The *lamiai* are modeled on Lamia, who is also known as a North African serpent Goddess, and are described as coarse-looking with the lower bodies of serpents. It is as a serpent that Lamia is linked to the Greek Medusa. In the folklore of modern day Greece, it is said that when a child has died of an unknown cause that the child has been strangled by the *lamiai.*

Lilith and the *lamiai* are related to a large number of so-called "birth demons," the spirits of women who have either died in childbirth or given birth to stillborn children. In their grief and rage, they, like Lilith, Lamia, and the *lamiai*, prey on the children of mortal women and their mothers. Among them are: the Malaysian *langsuyar*, the Indonesian *pontianak*, the Aztec *cihuapipiltin*, and the Greek *strix* or *strige.* More modern images of these birth demons can still be found in *La Llorona* of Mexico and the American southwest, the banshee of Ireland and the White Lady of Europe.

Empusa, by some accounts the daughter of the goddess Hecate, is also said to be a demonic creature who, like Lilith, can transform herself into a beautiful young woman in order to seduce men as they sleep. *Empusae*, the class of demons associated with Empusa, could enter the body of their prey to eat its flesh and drink its blood. *Lamiai*, *empusae*, and *lilim* (the demon children born of Lilith) all came to be general names for a range of bloodsucking witches or demons.

Not all goddesses are remembered as only witches, demons or child-eaters. Some say that Isis, a winged goddess of healing and nurturing, was the model for modern-day angels. The virgin mother of Horus and the "Giver of Life," she was later identified with the virgin Mary and the development of the cult of the Madonna and child. As the "Giver of Life," she could also bring the dead back into the world of the living, as she did with her consort Osiris. Anyone who has read Anne Rice's *The Vampire Lestat* knows the legends of Isis and Osiris and how Isis gathered the pieces of Osiris' dismembered body and breathed life back into them. In Whitley Strieber's best-selling novel *The Hunger*, Miriam is one of the Egyptian ancients who, in her modern-day life, uses a blade formed in the shape of an ankh, the symbol of divine and everlasting life, to spill the blood of her victims. The ankh also represents sexual union and the union of the male and female principles, as do the joined symbols of Yin and Yang.

If we revision the dark angel, embrace the aspects of sexuality, blood, death—all that we are taught to deny and fear—what does our new angel look like? The followers of Kali believe that it is essential to face the terror of death as well as the beauty of life. What if, when we look death in the eye, we see not the horrific figure of death that we are taught to expect, but the beauty of death when it comes to us in its natural form?

The stories in *Dark Angels* suggest a portrait of these shadow selves. The angel may truly be a dark angel, the traditional vampire: the wanton woman whose sexuality brings destruction, the cruel and terrifying woman as death personified, the woman whose need leads to a wasting away of those around her. The angel may also appear as the virgin Goddess in her ancient form, whose sexuality was held sacred and with whom sex was a form of divine union. The vampire is also the death angel, an aspect of the wisewoman, the hag or the crone—the dark moon Goddess who receives the dead into her womb and prepares them for rebirth.

"The Countess Visonti" is an excerpt from the novel *Sardia: A Story of Love* (1891). *Sardia* was written by Cora Linn Daniels, a Victorian folklorist and occultist. In the character of Sybil Visonti, Daniels creates the classic vamp: the dark, sensuous, serpentine woman who unscrupulously and unrepentantly uses her sexuality to destroy both men and women. Ralfe, who is one of many in love with Sybil, describes her:

> What a woman! How that dark, fascinating face, with its eyes of velvet flame, passionate, humid, glowing flashing...the lips that breathed a peculiar music in every tone, the arms that seemed to always long to embrace, the strangely moving hands which made such subtly expressive gestures, adding an undulating and rhythmic grace to every tender word...rushed upon his sight, and even in imagination almost blinded him.

Guy, Lulu's fiancé, warns her against Sybil. He describes her as a "fascinating, dangerous, subtle woman" who has "arts that no innocent woman can know." He tells her that Sybil is "a vampire.... She eats one up body and soul."

"Blood Wedding" is a contemporary story that shares the setting and sensibilities of Daniels' "The Countess Visonti." Set in 1882, the proper ladies and gentlemen of British society are shocked and dismayed, and also rather titillated, by the exotic nature of Sir Percy's foreign-born bride. Even as they are alarmed and tittering behind Miriam's back, the young men fantasize about dressing up their "whores" to look like her. Victorian sensibilities are evident throughout: the tightly controlled eroticism, the glimpse of something forbidden, Antoinette's innocent submission to her husband's "duty." At the same time, the new Victorian technology—transfusion—is introduced, much as it was in Bram Stoker's *Dracula.* In Stoker's day, transfusion was a major breakthrough in medical technology. Percy's willingness to give Miriam regular transfusions of blood gives her a normal life and social acceptability. Antoinette offers her pleasures of another sort.

In Amelia G's "Wanting," Danielle, an urban vampire with a gothic/glam rock past, is out of place in a small, rural town. Rachel recognizes Danielle, and remembers her prancing on stage in black netting and a pair of black leather wings, a "gothic wet dream." Reaching beyond Danielle's dirty black trench coat and her glitter rock past, Rachel finds much more than Danielle's "death angel" stage persona. Danielle brings pleasure, not pain, as soft and smooth and supple as the wings of an angel.

Medea, in her goddess aspect, is female wisdom, the source of the art of healing. Some say that Medea is the daughter of Hecate, who is herself related to the Egyptian midwife goddess, Heqit. In Greek mythology, Medea was the wife of Jason, who took another lover and drove Medea mad. In her madness, Medea killed her children to punish Jason for his betrayal. In "Medea" by Carol Leonard, Medea is a midwife named for the goddess midwife. In the story, Medea is from a long line of midwives who honor women's regenerative power and their wise-blood through ancient rituals of blood-drinking. Hannah has literally dreamed of these rituals. When Hannah finally meets Medea, Medea devours Hannah, and Hannah is born anew into the mysteries and wisdom of the Mother.

It is the loss of a child that brings Marian face to face with the vampire goddess Lamia in Thomas Roche's "Orphans." Before Lamia was reduced to a she-demon, she was a Libyan serpent goddess who guided the soul through the underworld. Lamia was known as "She Who Gives Life to the Dead." Roche describes Lamia as "the protector of all spiritual orphans, who devours their souls to protect them from the forces that would otherwise destroy them, and keeps them safe until...they can survive in the world again." In his story "Orphans," the serpent goddess Lamia is restored to her ancient mysteries. Marian, bearing the burden of her grief as well as the grief of her lover, Catherine, unknowingly enters the lair of the serpent Goddess. Lamia guides Marian through the darkness and back into the light, using ritual bloodletting and blood-sharing to restore Marian's faith and Catherine's soul.

Melanie Tem's "Presence" brings to mind the image of the triple Goddess: the maiden, mother and crone. Like the virgins of old, she is one unto herself. She loses herself in the mysteries of blood, sex and the divine mother. As she ages, she comes to see herself surrounded by "women's eyes...friendly eyes; seductive eyes." The eyes, perhaps, of the dark moon Goddess, ready to take her in, transform her, and make her one with the mysteries of life and the universe.

Death also seduces the eager and willing Sara in "Daria Dangerous" by Shawn Dell. Sara finds not only death, but also consolation in the arms of Daria, "her killer, her mother, her lover." Daria is a modern-day vamp, a lesbian biker goddess who once rode with a girl gang called the Sirens. Daria, like Kali, embodies life and death. She brings salvation through sensuality and liberation by coming face to face with death.

Death without life is the theme of much of Alejandra Pizarnik's work. Pizarnik, the child of Jewish immigrant parents to Argentina, committed suicide in 1972. Her obsession with death is evident in much of her work. One critic suggests that she regarded herself "as an outsider, apart from the realm of the living." In "The Bloody Countess," Pizarnik uses fiction to create a near-journalistic account of the life and obsessions of the Countess Erzebet Bathory, a sixteenth-century Hungarian noblewoman who tortured and killed an estimated six hundred young women in her employ. Bathory became legendary for her cruelty, and the myths and legends suggest that she had been a vampire. There is significant evidence to indicate that Bram Stoker relied heavily on the history of the Countess to create his Hungarian Count Dracula. Pizarnik's stark and vivid accounts of the Countess who, in her absolute boredom, must create even more cruel and unusual forms of torture to extract pain and suffering from her victims in order to feel anything herself are haunting.

Life without death is the curse of Cecilia Tan's vampire in "The Tale of Christina." Jillian's desire for something she can never truly have is fraught with self-destruction. Her single-minded desire encompasses all else; her desire is so intense that it swallows her whole. When Christina begs Jillian to turn her into a vampire, Jillian explains that it is the desire that can never be attained, the need that can never be satiated that dooms one to be a vampire. If the need can be met, if the desire can be quenched, the possibility of being a vampire cannot exist. In having been consumed by her own desire, Jillian has become the ultimate vampire.

The vampire of Renee Charles' "Cinnamon Roses," like "The Tale of Christina" and "Orphans," exists in the nether world of the gothic rock subculture. This vampire, however, faces a mundane world of some rather familiar, down-to-earth concerns—keeping a job, paying the rent, getting her next meal. A hairdresser by trade, razors and clippers ease the concern about where her next meal might be coming from.

The consuming aspect of the vampire is one of the most widely recognized. The traditional vampire is driven by her need for blood and, in sacrificing all else for that need, she loses her soul. What if the vampire can manage her desire, control her appetite, if you will? In Lawrence Schimel's "Femme-de-Siècle," we see a somewhat lighter side of the consuming vampire. Her butch lover is worried that her newly-found love has an eating disorder. Of course, she doesn't suspect that her Geena Davis femme is a vampire whose mortal concerns for her "figure" keep her on a continual "diet" of anemic blood.

The vampire is a passionate creature, consumed by its desires and by its appetite. Essentially a sexual creature, the vampire is as likely to seduce her intended victim as to attack. The image of penetration of the flesh by fangs, the lapping up of blood with the tongue—each of these images, and many more, have been interpreted and reinterpreted in the language of sex. The vampire is carnal—it is about flesh and blood. It is about the body and its attachment to this world, about attraction and repulsion, and about how the flesh, even our own, can both compel us and betray us. The traditional image of the vampire, like the traditional image of Lilith as described by Raphael Patai in *The Hebrew Goddess*, is "the embodiment of everything that is evil and dangerous in the sexual realm."

In *Mysteries of the Dark Moon: The Healing Power of the Dark Goddess*, Demetra George writes that "both men and women need to examine, heal, and transform their unconscious fears of being destroyed by sexual energies." In reimagining the Goddess, we also reimagine our selves and our relationship to the world. In reimagining the vampire, we see that our folklore isn't static—we define it as much as it defines us. Perhaps that is why the vampire continues to be so popular. In embracing the vampire, we are embracing our shadow selves, our brightest hopes as well as our darkest desires. The vampire in each of us reminds us that we are human after all.

Pam Keesey

Minneapolis
July 1995

Wanting

AMELIA G

I WAS SURPRISED when the DJ said that last rockin' number was off the new Motley Crüe album. Gotta love that nouveau underground sound. Well maybe. Then the DJ added that Madison is in the video for "Hooligan's Holiday," the song we had just heard. Like anyone in this part of the country knows who Madison is. Made me wish we got cable around here.

I was guiding my monstrous old Caddie along the route to the grocery store, when the DJ turned on The Cult's "Fire Woman." I blame that—maybe credit that—for everything that came after. I gave a guy passing in a pickup the one-finger salute just in case he was thinking my car was too big for a woman. Never look down on anyone in a vehicle big enough to take you out without slowing down.

I'm old enough to remember seeing Southern Death Cult live. I was spending three years abroad. Pissing my parents off. They'd pissed me off with their reaction to 'Cilla. "It's not your fault, honey. It's a sickness." *Please.* I'd charged the plane tickets on my mother's platinum AmEx and made my dramatic gesture. Such a rebel. Ha. Now, at thirty-two, I can see that if I had really loved 'Cilla, I would have stuck around. But hindsight is always 20/20. Besides, true drama would have been a one-way ticket.

As I got off the country highway and turned onto the street that led into town, fucking Pearl Jam came on the radio. So I turned it off. The money had just about run out so I knew I was going to have to return to the world soon. Contract out with Oribé. Do fashion or something. I had made the transition from Goth to glam without pain. I may be the only person on the planet who enjoyed "Fire Woman" as much as "God's Zoo." But the thought of doing makeup in a grunge world made me ill.

A comfortably warm, clean springtime evening, the sort that can only be found in upstate New York, was just beginning to settle in around the town. I parked outside the market.

I noticed her immediately after stepping across the threshold of the store. Maybe it was her coat. I'm not sure. I was only slightly chilly in my tank top and cut-offs, but she had her shoulders hunched under a dirty leather trench coat. She was pale. Sickly-looking really. But the shock of recognition was sharp and fast. There was no mistaking the perfect arch of those thin eyebrows, those unnaturally angular cheekbones, the thin upper lip contrasting with her pouting lower one. Begging for deep red lipstick. Begging for something. She was small and thin and ludicrously out of context next to the fresh strawberry display.

"Danielle?" I asked incredulously, although I knew it was she.

"How do you know my name?" the waif asked.

My heart sank. I'd only done her makeup a few times. She had been more a part of the whole glam thing, while I'd hung out mostly on the Gothic scene. There was no real reason she should remember me more than a decade later. "You are Danielle Hazzard, aren't you?"

She smiled thinly, but with humor. "Danielle Jones now. Did I know you then?"

I held my hand out. "Rachel Bloom. Pleased to remake your acquaintance. I, uhm, did your makeup for you a couple of times. When you warmed up for Hanoi Rocks."

Her hand was cool to the touch and she left it in mine a beat longer than appropriate. "Opening for that band was so terrific. So terrifying. They were so good. Omnisexual and androgynous. Michael was so beautiful. Is so beautiful. Almost enough to make you change your mind." Her voice was low and not quite accented, but not very American either. I wondered if the Michael comment was a test.

I took my hand back and I was about to hold forth on my opinion about standards for beauty being the same, regardless of gender. Then I caught sight of the shopkeeper watching us. I pretty much kept to myself, but the last thing I needed was to arouse any more comment than my reclusive lifestyle already did. "Would you like to go have a drink or something?" I asked Danielle.

"I don't really like to eat anyway." Danielle gestured around the little market disdainfully.

I couldn't remember what I'd needed to pick up. So I led her back out to my car.

"The black Cadillac. Is that one yours?"

"I'm a sucker for nice tail fins," I said, mentally raising my estimation of this woman who had been somehow conjured from my past.

Maybe it was my imagination, but as I opened the passenger door for her she seemed to wiggle for my benefit. "Nice tail fins are important," she replied. Not that I could really tell what her ass was like under that long muddy leather. It looked like she'd been slopping pigs in it. I swear there was even mud in her hair. "Aesthetics in general are important," Danielle added after we were both seated in the womb of my big black Cadillac. Funny words, given how she was dressed. I couldn't help thinking about the mud she had tracked into my car.

I started up the powerful engine of my car and felt it come to life, rumbling reassuringly beneath our seats. The mysterious creature sitting beside me turned and said, "You didn't go by Rachel Bloom ten years ago, did you?"

I blushed. "No."

"What name did you use?"

I guided the car back onto the main street of town and drove past the one sad little bar where four dusty pickups and a beat-up Pontiac sat outside. Even over the purr of my Caddie's motor, we could hear male laughter. A teenage boy was climbing out of the pickup with the least dust. "This is the only real place in town to get a drink." I pointed.

"Looks charming," she said sarcastically.

I stopped the car but didn't turn it off. "They water down all the good stuff," I told her. "I've got a better bar at home and I never even entertain."

"Let's go to your house, then."

I looked at her, but her expression was unreadable.

I put my monstrous motor back in motion. "Are you sure?" I said. I pointed to the boy going into the bar. "He's kind of cute." I waited for her response. Testing. Not even breathing.

She watched the boy's faded blue jeans and red plaid shirt with the sleeves ripped off, watched them disappear into the bar. "Don't they have a drinking age in America any more?"

I exhaled. Still unreadable. "It is a small town. The barkeep overlooks everything. It's hard enough for him to stay in business as it is. Besides, the sheriff is his brother-in-law."

Danielle said nothing, just hunched her shoulders and held herself.

"What do you want to do, Danielle?"

"Let's go sample some of your fine bar. I could really use a shower too. Then maybe you could do my makeup again."

Images from the last time I did her makeup flashed through my mind. I could barely concentrate on the road as the Caddie took us up the winding dirt road to my house. Danielle had been in a band which played music too bouncy to totally appeal to the Gothic audience. But she was a Gothic wet dream. She never stopped moving during a show, never ran out of energy as long as the crowd wanted more. She still looked cool, but it was odd to think of this sickly woman as that hyperactive girl who strutted across the stage in nothing but black netting and bat wings, seeming to feed off her audience's excitement.

I had hoped I'd get to do her wings, but she did her own costuming. Just liked getting a hand with the painting. I had loved accenting the planes of her angular face, but I had almost died of embarrassment when she asked me to rouge her nipples. My housemate who had gotten me backstage—she knew the guitarist—had almost died laughing. Danielle's perfect high round breasts did show in that outfit though. And the rouge made her nipples stand out through the black netting.

"So what name did you go by in England?" Danielle interrupted my reverie and I blushed at what I'd been thinking about.

Then I blushed at what I was about to tell her. "Uhm, Razor. Razor Flower."

"That's pretty."

"Yeah, pretty pretentious."

I stopped the car and Danielle gasped. "Is this your house?"

"No, I live in the servant's quarters." She looked at me, searched my face. "Yes, this is my house. Real estate is pretty cheap around here. Joys of living in the middle of fucking nowhere."

The gravel crunched under our feet as we walked across the driveway to the front steps. I let us in and showed Danielle the bath. It was a beautiful old thing with claw feet, but I'd had the plumbing modernized so the water could be wonderfully hot. And I had an eighty-gallon tank so I never ran out of hot water. Different luxuries are important to different people.

Hoping she would be naked when she got out of the tub, I waited for her in my bedroom. The country sun was setting as I laid my zillions of little jars of makeup out on the dressing table with the antique three-part mirror. I had just brought out two glasses of ice and a couple of bottles of my favorites, when Danielle entered the bedroom. Although she was even more pale without all the dirt on her, she looked a thousand times healthier. Her hair was blacker and longer than I had realized.

I wished she was not wearing my huge white terry cloth robe, but at least she had left those awful, muddy clothes in the bathroom. I forced myself to take a couple of scarves out of the dressing table drawer so I could pick one to tie her incredible hair away from her face. I forced myself to act like playing with makeup a little was all I wanted.

Her skin was warm from the bath as I ran my fingers over her face, using a combo of Bob Kelly purples and grays on her eyes. They were already big, but the makeup gave them a knowing look. I rimmed her eyes in blackest black. All makeup artists have their own little biases. Mine happens to be that I believe black eyeliner is the only one that counts, the only one that is ever genuinely in fashion.

As I worked, Danielle made casual conversation. We talked

about how much we had loved the dark bondage-inspired fashions of the early eighties, about how much we hoped that look was coming back in style. She asked me how I could afford such a mansion, even in upstate New York. I surprised myself by telling her the truth about my trust fund, about the lawsuit with my parents, that they'd said I wasn't competent. They just hadn't thought about what ten percent means when they'd offered the judge their proof.

"That's great," Danielle said, "the judge even awarded you punitive damages."

I used my index finger to stroke the red Chanel lipstick onto her smiling lips. It might have been my imagination, but I thought she licked my finger when I added the X-rated lip gloss as a top coat.

When those shiny red lips moved to say, "You should put some blusher on my nipples. Nobody does that like you do," it wasn't my imagination. She let the robe fall open just enough to reveal two coral tips of breasts that were far too high and too firm for the age she had to be. Maybe she'd had surgery. She didn't seem like an exercise freak.

I wanted her to admit that she wanted me before I risked anything, so I began to rouge her nipples with a nonchalance I had been unable to muster at twenty-one. "I thought you didn't remember me."

She moaned softly as her left nipple, then her right, grew stiff and hard between my blush-slick fingers. "I remember you. I guess I just wasn't thinking clearly." I decided that counted as enough of an admission of desire; I leaned forward and buried my face between her breasts. She smelled like gardenias, like my soap, and she moaned again when I kissed her there. "I'm usually fuzzy when I've just woken up," she added, "I like to sleep until there's really a need—really a need to do otherwise."

There was almost an electric shock when our lips met. I'd wanted to kiss her for so long. I'd wanted to kiss her so badly. Her tongue explored my mouth like a wild intruder, forcing my tongue back out from between her lips with her strength. She held me with a fierce urgency, tearing my tank top off over my head and dragging my shorts—then my little black silk panties—down to the floor.

"You've smeared your lipstick," I said when we finally came up for air. I reached a finger up to fix it.

"I don't want you distracted from your pleasure. Can I tie you up?" she whispered. Danielle's breathing was already heavy. It must have been even longer for her than it had been for me. "Please," she moaned, "if you like bondage, I know you'll like what I want to do."

"Okay." I nodded and picked up the scarves. Some part of me knew that this was why I had gotten them out, that this was what I wanted. I felt incredibly self-conscious and aware of every part of my body as I walked naked over to the double bed. Danielle, still in my terry cloth bathrobe, followed me. I handed her the scarves, lay down across the patchwork quilt, and held my wrists up to the redwood bedposts.

The bonds she tied around my wrists were quick but gentle. I tested them lightly and realized that the knots were perfect. I was firmly secured, but my blood would have no problem circulating.

"Do you want to be mine?" she whispered huskily.

I nodded.

"Do you want to be mine?" Her tone was sharper this time.

"Yes. Yes, I want you. I want to be yours."

"Give me your leg," she said, gripping my ankle. Once she had tied me spread-eagled on the bed, I felt incredibly vulnerable. The setting was so wholesome, so countrified. And there we were, two fair-skinned, dark-haired creatures of the night. How had I ended up out in the country?

She stroked her hand up my thigh.

"Oh...take off the robe."

"Later." She took an ice cube out of one of the glasses I had intended for drinks. She ran the ice up the thigh she had just stroked. "Do you like this?"

I moaned.

She ran the ice cube over my hip, along my tummy, up my rib cage, and circled my left nipple. It was instantly hard and aching. She ran the ice cube across my cleavage to the other nipple where it melted.

Danielle pulled another ice cube out of her glass and, without warning, plunged it into the place of need between my thighs. "Oh." I was so hot, it started melting fast. She took another piece of ice and ran it teasingly over my clit. I almost screamed, it was so intense. She ran the corner of the ice up over my body, then back down teasingly across my aroused clitoris, down across my lips, then lower. A cold damp puddle was forming on the quilt beneath my ass. I shivered with both chill and arousal.

She put a new ice cube into me. "Do you like that?" she breathed.

"So cold, so cold."

"Do you want me to stop?"

"No, no, don't stop." I thrashed around on the bed, my pelvis reaching for her. Her eyes had a mischievous glint, while her close-mouthed smile was driving me mad with lust. "Don't stop," I begged her, "I want you to go on. Take off the robe."

"Later." Danielle stuffed another ice cube into me. She was running another piece of ice from side to side, thigh to thigh, when she suddenly dropped her head, hiding my pelvis beneath her ebony hair. Her tongue burned on my clit and this time I did scream. Her name. Incoherent sounds. And, I think, her name again. The top of her rough tongue scraped a sweet circle of intense sensation. I was coming so hard, I nearly blacked out.

Danielle lay down next to me on the crazy flowered quilt. She held me, but she made no move to untie me. "Do you always come like that?" she murmured. She sounded sated herself.

"Only when I'm as turned on as you make me." We lay together for a moment. Then I asked, "Did you come too?"

"Mmm-hmm," she replied, smiling lazily. "You're so responsive. It's really beautiful. It's really exciting."

"You'd like it better with your skin on mine," I said. "I want to taste you."

"You promise it will be okay?" she asked. The last remnants

of sunlight streaked through the lace curtains, highlighting her glossy tresses. She looked healthier now too. Still pale, but not in a bad way. And I wanted so badly to see her naked. So badly.

"I'm sure it will be okay," I told her as firmly as I could manage while tied to the bed.

She put her feet down on the wood floor and stood. Then, with a shy look, she shrugged off the white robe to expose the black leathery wings I had known she was hiding. "Are you sure it is okay?" she asked me.

"Let me prove to you how okay it is," I told her. "Let me please you."

"You please me already," Danielle answered, but she crawled up over me anyway and placed one stark white thigh on either side of my head.

I lifted my head and tasted her. I've been with a lot of women and before, whenever I heard honey metaphors, I always thought they were stupid. But Danielle...Danielle tasted like candy apples. "You're so sweet," I spoke into her mound.

"It really is okay with you." She laughed a small giggle of freedom and then, moaned.

"It's okay," I groaned between licks, "You're so beautiful, so sweet, so...so...I couldn't want you more if I tried." And I settled into pleasing her in earnest. All too quickly her little moans turned into a violent body-wracking shaking. She slid back down my body, her wetness affirming my power over her.

She enfolded us both in her dark wings and the leather was soft and smooth and supple and alive, not like her coat at all. I thought maybe I should be freaked out or something. Motley Crüe doing an industrial-influenced album would have been more surprising to me than her wings being real. "I'm turned on all over again," I told her. "Maybe not again. Maybe just still. I want you."

"What I want is your wanting. Do you want me?"

I opened my eyes and looked at her, her thin frame somehow managing to loom over me. "Yes, I want you. More than I've ever wanted anyone else."

She smiled. Open-mouthed, showing her fangs for the first

time. The fangs I had known were there. "Are you going to drink my blood?" I asked.

"No, silly." She threw her head back and her long heavy hair flew up into the air behind her and cascaded down over her shoulders onto my breasts like a black waterfall. She laughed and it was the most beautiful music I had ever heard. "What I need is your wanting. Just your wanting."

For a moment, I was almost disappointed, but my body always knows what I really want. And my body throbbed for her touch. "I want you. I want you so much. Please touch me. I'm almost there."

And, smiling, she reached down between my trembling thighs and stroked me in that last gentle circle I needed to put me over the edge.

My orgasm broke through me. The release was incredible, but the wanting didn't go away. And neither did Danielle.

Blood Wedding

GARY BOWEN

THE BRIDE wore red. Crimson velvet, the color of men's blood, and the texture of women's skin. She was a tall bride, made even taller by her lofty headdress decked in pearls, the long ropes hanging low on her breast, five strands suspended from the edge of the hat, exotic, erotic, undeniably foreign, a sensation among the tightly trussed ladies and gentlemen of 1882....

Outrageous, outlandish, how could Sir Percy select such a barbaric person to be the Wife of Lestley Hall? Russian, she was; backwards, feudal, anachronistic, a museum mannequin from the fourteenth century walking through the modern parlor, the skirts of her long dress rustling against the furniture with a susurration that was almost lascivious.

All the nephews and their gentlemen friends were following her with their eyes, tongues darting nervously over their lips, wondering if, when next they visited the brothels, they could pay the whores to get themselves up like that, but what whore could afford so many pearls? They were her dowry, ten thousand pounds sterling, made into a dozen different headdresses; necklaces and bracelets added to her splendor, rattling softly against each other where they weighed down her wrists, their luster gleaming in the gaslight, her alabaster skin whiter than they, while two points of vivid color glowed on her cheeks, natural, not rouge, for she needed no cosmetic help. Perhaps it was the heat of so much velvet that made her flush so, or perhaps—and this was whispered behind lace fans—she was ill. Consumption.

Heads nodded genteelly so as to not disturb elaborate chignons. Yes, he had taken her straight to the doctor when they arrived in London; the prognosis was not good. She was deathly ill. Then, with respectability imposed by imminent death, they smiled indulgently at her, poor thing, not long for this world, her mind unraveling from the strain of it. And Sir Percy! What gallantry! To wed the woman anyhow, attending to her every motion, serving her whatever she asked. After the suitable two-year mourning period, some other bride would wear the pearls, reset according to prevailing notions of good taste and propriety. So the ladies smiled their bright, feral smiles at the Wife of Lestley Hall, plotting how they would remake her husband and her fortune when she was dead and buried.

Sir Percy, hair so pale as to be colorless under the gaslight, was perspiring lightly over his tight collar, black tuxedo fitting smoothly over a lean body (he had lost weight while in Russia, but English cooking would soon fatten him up again), while he introduced his bride to whomever happened to be at hand. She had not only refused a church wedding, choosing to be wed instead in the Great Hall, but had also refused to have a reception line and now everyone was milling about in chaos trying to extend their congratulations, if not their good will.

"Antoinette and Marcus Culpepper. Marcus is my business partner...."

"Antoinette!" The crimson bride spoke warmly; the pearls seemed almost too heavy for her extended hands. "I am delighted to make your acquaintance. I know no one here, and since you are the wife of Dear Percy's business partner, I am sure we will spend much time together." Her voice was rich with unexpected depths that made her sound totally foreign, though in fact her English was quite good.

Antoinette, pale and demure in a dove gray gown with a bosom covered in falls of white lace, let her one hand be clasped by the two pearl-laden hands, and smiled nervously at this strange creature who was inevitably going to be part of her social circuit. "I'm delighted to meet you, Miriam. I'm sure we'll be good friends," though she could not believe it.

Marcus, dark as his wife was pale, and portly as Percy was

lean, smiled indulgently. "My wife's got excellent taste! She'll take you round to all the best shops and you'll be fitted up English style in no time!"

The bride smiled coolly at him. "I am not English, and I do not intend to follow the English fashion." Then to Antoinette, "Will you walk in the garden with me? The heat is making me faint." She still held Antoinette's hand in hers, and before the younger woman could organize a suitable reply, the bride drew her away.

"They're hitting it off famously," Marcus' voice boomed behind them.

The evening was cool and pleasant, with the faintest perfume of apple blossoms upon the breeze. The moon shone brilliant and distant above the neatly manicured lawns, which rolled over swells and swales between the park and the orchard, with a lake at the bottom of the property. The great horseshoe drive was full of carriages, their drivers sleeping on the boxes (or if they thought they could get away with it, in the carriage itself), or standing idly smoking while the grand folks entertained themselves inside.

Gravel crunched under Antoinette's feet, uncomfortable through the thin soles of her dancing slipper. Inadvertently pressing closer to her strange hostess, she shrank away from the servants who turned to stare at the two women. "Perhaps we should use the rear garden," she ventured.

"The lake is most refreshing," Miriam replied. "But you must know that. I'm sure you've been here before."

"Why yes, on a few occasions. Percy had a house party every summer."

A little white folly stood on the shore above the lily pads, great lotus-like blossoms ethereal above the green-black, placid water. The grass underfoot was slicked with dew, and chilled Antoinette's feet. She lifted her skirts hesitantly, afraid the lackeys might get a glimpse of her ankles, but not wanting to wet the dress. Miriam had released her hand, and strode down the lawn before her, and it was either stand still and be stranded alone in the midst of that green expanse like a statue in the moonlight, or follow after. So she followed.

The steps of the folly faced the lake, and Miriam sank down upon the second step, her hands lifting the headdress off her hair. Her black hair was coiled in a braid piled on top of her head, wound with strands of pearl, and had been covered and hidden by the headdress. She loosed the pins and the long braid fell over her shoulder.

"Sit beside me," she said patting the step. "Is not the lake beautiful? The lilies are like little green islands in a silver sea."

Antoinette daintily maneuvered herself onto the step beside the bride, wondering when was the last time she had sat upon a step. She had knelt upon the grass while cutting flowers from her garden, but that was not quite the same thing. Next to her the Wife of Lestley Hall was a cool presence, even though their bodies nearly touched. Antoinette shifted a bit uncomfortably on account of her corset, then realized that her companion was naturally slim, and had not bound her waist. It astonished her, for she took it for granted that however small a waist a woman might be, she would want it smaller, and corsets were the answer. She shifted yet again, the step not lending itself to her tight-laced comfort, and accidentally bumped against the woman.

Miriam put her arm about Antoinette's waist, a forward gesture that seemed entirely expected from such a foreign person. Antoinette sat stiffly upright, wishing that she had thought to slip upstairs and loosen her stays a bit, then she laughed softly and relaxed a bit.

"Yes?" asked Miriam.

"I was just wishing my corset was not so tight." She never would have said such a thing to her other lady friends, but somehow she knew the other woman would not be shocked by such an admission.

Miriam smiled. "I never wear them. We have them in Russia, you know. We are not so backwards as you English believe. It is only that I have chosen to live so ostentatiously. Though," she admitted, "such ostentation does come more naturally to the Russian character than the English."

"You are a most extraordinary person."

Miriam laughed. "More extraordinary than you know." Miriam's fingers played with the loose strands of hair at the nape of Antoinette's neck. A frisson went down her spine, and she shuddered, scarcely knowing what to think, or what she was feeling.

The fingers played against her neck, nails scratching lightly so that the most bizarre heat shot through her veins. "What are you doing?" she whispered.

Miriam drew her nail along Antoinette's spine. "Teasing you. You like it, no?"

"I...don't know."

The nail traced the delicate collarbone, pausing in front in the notch.

"Is Marcus satisfying in bed?"

"He does his duty," she whispered.

"His duty," the other repeated. "And pleasure?"

"It is a wife's duty to submit."

"But it is a pleasure too, or so it should be."

Antoinette trembled violently. "We should not talk of such things."

"Because we are ladies? Men talk of such things all the time, comparing their mistresses to their wives. Even your Marcus."

"I cannot believe it!"

Miriam shrugged. "All men are like that. Women are different."

"Yes," she replied reluctantly, but she had to admit it was true.

"Women sit and look at lakes, and talk of forbidden things."

"If you say so," she felt weak and almost ill, while the finger drifted down her pale breast to fetch up against the lace decked edge of her cleavage. Then the dark head bent, and pressed a soft kiss against her flesh; a small pinprick made her gasp. Then the sensations rushing through her made her lightheaded and she dropped back onto her elbows, heaving breast close under the red lips, which suckled gently against her breast.

"Let me loosen your corset." Miriam helped her to sit up, and unhooked the back of her dress, sleeves falling partly down her arms.

What will Marcus say? What if the servants are watching?

But they were sitting below the folly, and it screened them from the drive, though if one of the drivers was minded to take a walk, he might discover them. The laces unknotted, Antoinette breathed more easily, grateful for the relief, and looked at the other woman in confusion. Then Miriam retied her corset in the looser position, and hooked up her dress again. She sat more easily upon the step, feeling both relieved and disappointed. Only then did she collect herself enough to look down at her bosom, and saw the small risen welt, like a bee sting upon her breast. She rubbed it gently, surprised to find it numb, and looked questioningly at her companion.

"I don't understand."

"Did you enjoy it?"

Something had drained from Antoinette, something containing shame and scruples and proper etiquette. "Yes, I did."

Miriam caught her beneath the chin. "Women are creatures of the head, while men are creatures of the flesh. It is our mouths that give us pleasure, and it is our brains that choose to whom we give our mouths."

Then her mouth closed over Antoinette's; ruby lips sealed against hers in a kiss that was both chaste and erotic. Antoinette closed her eyes, swooning against the bride, no thought in her mind at all except, *No man ever kissed me like that.*

The kiss went on for a very long time, mouth pressing mouth, then a sharp tongue touched against the sensitive flesh of her lips, and they parted without any volition on her part.

She felt the prick of the tongue, sharp as a stinger, then numb against her own tongue, and felt the languor stealing through her limbs for a second time, and understood that this was something Miriam had done to her, something beyond her ability to understand. A crimson arm supported her back, and her head lolled against the velvet shoulder while she lay lost as if in a laudanum dream from which she never wanted to awaken.

When Miriam lifted her head Antoinette slowly opened her eyes, long lashes dark against the pallor of her skin. She lifted a weak hand to the other woman's face, and said, "No wonder Percy loves you so."

"I owe Percy a great debt," Miriam replied meditatively. "It is his English medicine that has saved me from the madness of my illness."

Antoinette drew herself up with great effort. "Are you ill? I had heard the rumor...."

"Dr. Blair experiments upon me. He runs a tube from Percy's arm to mine, and Percy's bright blood enters my veins. Then I am better for a few days, a week even. We have tried to find others who might lend me their blood, but each of them has made me ill. Dr. Blair thinks it is a nervous reaction, that I am too distressed to accept the blood of strangers, and can only accept the donation of one dear to me. Perhaps he is right."

Antoinette's eyes were huge in the luminous night. "How horrible! How awful! I can imagine how frightened you must be, and how glad you must be to have Percy at your side!"

Miriam caressed her chin. "Not just Percy."

Antoinette flushed, then her startled eyes met Miriam's. "Me?"

"If you would."

Antoinette was lost. "I cannot...."

Miriam smiled gently. "I thought not." She rose to her feet, bound her hair back upon her head and replaced the headdress. Antoinette scrambled to her feet.

"Miriam...."

"I'm sure we will meet again some day." She began to walk with long strides up the hill.

Antoinette pressed fingers against her lips, then ran after her, picking up her skirts, ankles flashing under the froth of petticoats. "Wait! Please wait!"

Miriam hesitated a moment, and Antoinette caught up with her. "I'll do it. I am terrified, but I'll do it."

Miriam's eyes sparkled with light, and she embraced her, gently kissing her cheek as a sister might. "Dear Antoinette, thank you." And in her ear she whispered, "I have so many secrets to share with you."

Presence

MELANIE TEM

MIRROR LOVINGLY angled between her legs. Tongue retracted and curled deep up against her soft palate. Trickle and drop from the inside of her elbow on the edges of her front teeth; baby teeth, milk teeth replaced by longer, sharper, permanent canines and incisors.

There were many things she could do for herself. Pleasurable things, painful things. There were things, though, that could only happen with another person.

She and her cousin would lie together on the fold-out sofa and trace their nails ever so lightly across the downy skin of each other's backs, the velvet skin of each other's arms. Sometimes they would prick; once she gouged.

Her cousin had breasts when she didn't. They made up a game: taking turns, they flattened the little mounds with the heels of their hands and squealed with delight when the breasts rebounded. They both thought the pink nipples looked like flowers, like flowering blood.

Her cousin's period started before hers did. She was the one to discover it. Trailing fingertips in scallops and stars along the inside of her cousin's thigh, she found the blood and kept her fingers there a while before she brought them up to show and exclaim. Her cousin was outraged. They did not spend the night together again.

She was eighteen, no longer jailbait. He was a virgin, too, barely eighteen himself, though nobody had ever referred to him as jailbait. Neither of them knew quite what to expect. They fumbled and despaired and laughed at themselves until they found ways to fit together: Penis into vagina, which was more uncomfortable than arousing. Tongues inside each other's mouths, which teased but did not satisfy. Teeth into the soft spot at the clasp of his clavicle, and just a little blood, which he didn't appear to notice she'd taken and which promised more than she knew, yet, how to accept.

After a while he moved awkwardly beside her and whispered in her ear, "Where did you go?"

"When?"

She felt his shyness. "When you—came."

She was somewhat surprised to hear him refer to a discrete, namable event. It had been such a diffuse sensation that she wasn't at all sure what had happened. "You came, too," she said, carefully. "Didn't you?"

He nodded, impatiently, as if she ought to know. "I went with you right to the edge but then, it was like you went on over. Into another world or something."

"Silly." She laughed at him and hugged him for his youthful romanticism.

He was serious, peering at her across the stiff motel pillow. "You went away from me and I couldn't find you. I couldn't follow you." Accusing. Alarmed.

She pledged: "I'll never go away from you." But of course she did.

In college, she put herself in the company of as many different kinds of people as she could. Immersed herself.

A bearded man and a woman with waist-length blond hair sang together. It was always unclear, presumably on purpose, whether they were lovers, but clearly there was love between them. Passion.

She sat in their audiences and studied the way their eyes locked, their melodies flowed together. The way they drew from each other. At the end of her junior year, the man transferred to another school, and the woman sang alone or with someone else.

Her academic advisor left his wife of twenty years for a man in the senior class who had attracted no one else's attention. She had been in countless classes with the two of them and had been aware of nothing between them. The younger man graduated and moved away. The advisor neither went with his lover nor went back to his wife. In his office, consulting with him about her senior thesis, she could see through him, the network of blood vessels to his brain and heart, the array of books on his shelves.

There were orgies. People fed each other whipped cream and strawberry jello. People fornicated in ways they imagined to be highly inventive. Pipes were passed. Mushrooms, tiny blotter squares and needles were shared. Various bodily fluids were sucked, ejaculated, exuded, swallowed, absorbed. Boundaries and barriers melted, but so did centers, so centers were never touched.

She studied. She read books. She practiced deep-breathing exercises and yoga, visualization and meditation. She took a course in hypnosis.

She made herself minutely aware of objects: the heaviness of a small round stone in the palm of her hand; the bright shadow of a flagpole angling up and over a sunny brick wall; the contrast and complement of blue sky and green tree, yellow sky and black tree, black sky and silver moonlit tree; the swish of tires on wet pavement under her window before dawn; the taste of oranges, chocolate, vanilla straight from the bottle, blood. The smell of blood.

Studying philosophy, she consciously tried to surrender to her own subconscious to the great Collective Unconscious, and thrilled to discover the original metaphorical definition of *schizophrenia,* which seemed to respect the mysteries of perception: "a state of mind so much in another realm that it *appears as if* split."

Studying poetry, writing some, she experienced the world as metaphor, experienced herself as extended metaphor with no clear referent.

"I can't keep up with you," her lover complained. "Everything turns you on."

"Not everything," she told him with a smile. "But I'm working on it."

"It's not fair. You come and come and come, and you feel it all over your body. I come once, if I'm lucky, and the sensation is localized."

She could think of nothing relevant to say. Her teeth did not taste of his blood, for he had pushed her away to speak his mind.

"Women lose themselves in sex. Literally," he went on, his indignation gathering. "Literally. They go off into some other dimension. Their consciousness is expanded. It must be a real trip."

Having smoked with him and with others and by herself, done acid and mescaline, she knew what he meant. She had felt the earth turning in space, the wind blowing inside her head. But she had always felt held back, confined.

They tried to make love again, but it was too soon for him. Now, as if in compensation, he let her nip the flesh under his ear. When she stilled from her climax—which had been only partial, a brink she could not yet go over—he was watching her resentfully from the other side of the bed, as if she knew something he could ever know.

They had proclaimed that there was no reason for them ever to break up. They loved each other so much and gave each other so much space. But before long there was simply nothing between them anymore except space, and they hadn't thought of that.

For a while she thought she might be frigid. Re-reading Freud, she considered: What *did* she want? Thinking about the implications of a *total* orgasm, she decided she had never had one.

She instructed herself that the concept of frigidity was another tool of masculine domination. She told herself that the idea of losing oneself in sex, of being transported to another realm, was ridiculous hyperbole, intended to make things seem more than they were.

At twenty-four, she married a man who didn't much like sex, who really didn't like to be touched at all. When he said he loved her, she was astonished. Later she couldn't remember what she'd said in return, what she'd been thinking; she could remember being in his arms, the distant affection with which he regarded her, and it seemed to her that she must have lost some time and space to him, or him to her, like liquid siphoned from one vein into another.

He never again held her willingly or told her that he loved her. She persuaded herself that he did, in his own way. On the infrequent occasions when they made love, she was so frantic to touch him that she never really touched him or herself at all.

He stayed up late until he knew she would be asleep. She rose early, knowing he would not be awake for hours yet. Alone in bed, alone in the long bright mornings, she would kiss the back of her own hand, the veined inside of her wrist. She would sink her teeth in.

They were married for almost five years, and when she left, he didn't seem to notice. After the initial sadness had subsided, she didn't notice much, either.

She was thirty-four, thirty-five, thirty-six. Her body and mind seemed in some ways to be settling, in some ways to be rising. She felt ready, and wary. More and more, she found herself choosing to love women; women bled.

For the first time she became aware of the closing of options. It no longer seemed to her that she could have everything. Her very life, every day of her life, was a choice among choices.

For the first time, she wanted to have a baby. The desire came on her as suddenly as conception itself: bland untroubled space one moment, a wildly multiplying cell the next.

She imagined new life inside her, assuming form, assuming spirit. She conceived of life flowing from one dimension into another, from one medium to another to another. She offered her own cells, her own flesh and blood. She willed her body to be a vessel, a conduit, a garden.

It was not. She did not become pregnant. More than one of her lovers said to her during those years, "You've got to let go. Nothing will ever happen for you if you don't learn to let go." She hadn't told any of them that she wanted to have a baby.

They were talking about something else: the disappointment they felt in her, the control.

Then suddenly, the baby took root. She didn't know who the father was, which pleased her. She didn't know the instant the sperm entered the ovum, as she imagined she would.

The baby was a metaphor, like black trees against a silver moonlit sky. Her sickness, her heaviness, the quiet brown spotting were not the essence of the thing, the thing-as-itself.

The baby grew inside her for almost three months. Then one day, there was a large amount of blood, a small amount of pain, and the baby was gone.

She touched her fingers to the blood and tissue the baby left behind. She touched her fingers to her lips.

She was forty-two when her lover whispered to her, mouth against her labia, labia against her mouth, "We fit together nicely, don't we? It's almost like making love to yourself."

She was forty-five when her lover's menstrual blood flowed out across her pillow. She couldn't get away from it. She couldn't take it in fast enough, deeply enough.

She was forty-eight when her lover bared her neck and guided her mouth there, held her mouth there, crooning.

This love lasted almost half as long as the life she lived when it began, almost a third of her life by the time it was over. They stayed together because of the blood, of course, because of their sharing of blood, their giving and taking of blood, their savoring blood and letting blood flow. But it was more than that.

She was sixty when her partner died. They had been together for nearly twenty years. There was so much blood she lost most of it, and her partner went somewhere while she stayed behind.

As she grew older, she seemed to grow into herself, and at the same time to grow away. She learned to be alone, and to value the loneliness.

Stripping woodwork in her two-hundred-year-old house, she began to see movement out of the corner of her eye. Feminine movement: a sturdy haze of blood that did not come from a wound.

Reading alone in her bedroom night after night, she began to see women's eyes at the window. Friendly eyes, seductive eyes. Just waking, just drifting off to sleep, she began to taste blood, then to savor it.

Finally, nearing seventy, she invited the presences in, and they accepted. They took up residence. They fed from her, teeth and tongues like the ghost of teeth and tongues. They brought her their blood. Her periods had stopped long ago, but her blood still flowed, and they matched their cycles to hers.

She walked in the mountains and the mountains possessed her, but briefly, briefly, and then she was herself again, climbing sheer stone.

Her mind began to travel. Tugging at its moorings all the time now, occasionally her consciousness would slip out of her body and watch herself with affectionate interest. But her mind always came back, unbidden.

She began to meet lovers who knew what they were doing. She herself learned how much to drink, how to position her lover's fingers and mouths, how to arrange her mind in order to go as far as they could take her, which was never very far.

"You really enjoy yourself, don't you?" her lovers would say, almost angry, almost insulting.

Gasping, she would suddenly be aware of coming back from some distant place. She would press her lips together then, as though to hold what she had managed to take, and would put out her hands and touch her lover, who often seemed to be turning away.

"You leave me," her lovers complained. "You go someplace I can't follow you. Maybe it's because you're so much older. Maybe you've learned something I don't know yet."

Then, having learned so little of what she wanted to learn, she would do what she could for them. Kiss them. Press her tongue inside. Bite. But it was never enough.

Gradually, the world showed itself to be not unreal, but incomplete. Sitting in her chair, staring at the lights or at the darkness in the glass, and she knew she was talking to herself. The frailty of her body, the glimmering of her mind possessed her, but briefly, briefly, and then she would have to take care of herself again.

She was eighty-two, eight-three. She had no interest in taking care of herself, but something kept pulling her back. Some pulse. Some circulation.

"You leave me. You go someplace I can't follow."

"She's senile. She doesn't know what's going on."

"Women lose themselves in sex."

"You really enjoy yourself, don't you?"

"She used to have such a fine, inquiring mind."

"You come and come and come."

"Women bleed."

Then one instant, as suddenly as conception, her body convulsed. Her vision washed blood-red, sun-white. Her mind swung away from her body and went on its way. The presences possessed her, consumed her; they showed themselves to be her own. She did not come back.

The Countess Visonti

CORA LINN DANIELS

Beautiful as sweet!
And young as beautiful! And soft as young!
And gay as soft! And innocent as gay!

YOUNG

Find out the cause of this effect;
Or rather say the cause of this defect,
For this effect defective comes by cause.

HAMLET

SARDIA STOOD leaning against an urn of flowers by the great entrance one evening, while Guy by his side idly tapped him on the shoulder. They stood together in that attitude of unconscious confidence which needs no words to betray a mutual respect and affection. They were both watching two ladies who were gently moving over the grass, absorbed in low conversation.

Lulu, who was half encircled by the embracing arm of Sybil Visonti, had cheeks that were dotted by two bright hectic spots, while all the rest of her pretty face was unusually pale. Every moment or two she instinctively half thrust away the little dark hand that lay on her hip, yet she was so engaged in conversation that she did not persist. It was a nervous, unconscious movement, evidently not directed by the will.

Sardia suddenly turned a keen questioning glance on Guy and said, "Do you like to see that?"

Mr. Thorne looked amused and surprised. "Does a man like to look at the woman he loves? At two beautiful women displaying their prettiest charms? Oh, no! Of course not," and he laughed.

"If I loved a woman I would take care of her," his friend said in a cold, slow way.

Guy started up. "Is it chilly?" and he moved towards the house. "I will get a wrap."

"Stay. It is not chilly. Do you believe in animal magnetism, Guy? The power of one will over another? If you do not you cannot see those women from the same standpoint that I do. But is not Lulu thin, excitable, changed? Where is her blithe laugh? I miss it."

Guy looked troubled. "So do I. Yet I had not thought of it. And it is I who love her. Sardia, old fellow,—tell me, out with it. What do you mean?"

"I cannot better answer you than to tell you to watch. Open your eyes," and he sauntered off.

Guy fell into a deep reverie. The soft chatter of the voices kept up an accompaniment to his thought. He earnestly compared in his own mind what Lulu had been in the early summer, and what she was now.

Sardia's few words had reminded him of his own vague fears, which, strongly accented on the Visonti's first arrival, had been lulled to rest by contact with her inscrutable charm, and now he found his darling brought before him in a new light. She was no longer the gay, merry, light-hearted, laughing Lulu. She no longer spent her days in every possible out-door exercise: "wild" over horseback riding, having a craze for a tricycle, rowing her tiny hands brown and callous, only too happy when standing the living figure-head of his jolly sail boat and glorying in the rough weather or stiff breezes that tossed her like a plume. Where was the shout with which she raced downstairs, and when softly rebuked for being not quite lady-like, the smiling pout and coquettish defiance with which she sprang from his detaining arms? Where were the overflowing life and the madcap pranks with which she had assailed him and tortured him, leading him in a dance which only made him adore her more and more? Now he found her lying languidly in the library or on the long seats in the summer-house. She refused the beautiful twilight walks so dear to him, she was so tired. She lay back among the cushions of the boat and gazed dreamily across the waves, instead of insisting on minding the wheel. Her sweet temper had thrown out sudden flashes of anger and irritability—in a moment atoned for, to be sure, by a melancholy little prayer for forgiveness—why, had he been blind, deaf, dumb? Fool that he was, had it not been for Sardia, how long would his soul have been stupidly unmindful and unheeding? He rose from his seat on the step and walked swiftly towards the young women.

"Lulu, I want you," he said sharply.

The Visonti stopped in her walk, and Lulu gazed at him in a sort of unseeing way, as if her mind was so far off that she had not comprehended. For a moment the man and woman looked into each other's eyes with a singular intensity. If she read anything that was in his thoughts, it elicited only defiance in Sybil. She drew her arm closer about Lulu with a sort of possessive pressure and looking softly into her eyes, slowly moved her away, saying gently but significantly,

"Lulu, *I* want you."

It was a mockery so delicate and so well done that it left Guy standing there, unable to utter a word, although he literally shook from head to foot with a sudden tide of hot yet impotent rage. Yet what could he do? Here were two ladies chatting, and one playfully retained her companion. Was he to murder her on the spot? He felt like it. He went into the house and to his room, threw off his coat, put his heels on top of a chair-back and smoked. It was a long time before he rejoined the party. He did not know—why should he?—how in spite of the little episode of her first visit to Sybil's room, Lulu had almost immediately overlooked and forgotten her sudden disgust. The very next day she had been made so conscience-stricken by the extreme kindness of Miss Visonti, and had been so quietly laughed out of her "pretty anger" by her new friend, that she felt she had been absurdly annoyed. Sybil was so exquisitely thoughtful, so delicate, her devotion to Lulu was so unpretending, yet so certain, that it exercised a singular influence, a soft flattery to which her innocent heart yielded with gratitude. She began to know the charm of being sought—sought persistently, patiently, humbly. She began to feel that her love and friendship to this one woman at least was invaluable—possessing an exceptional preciousness. She felt that she possessed the key to a thousand times richer nature than her own. The magician made her believe that she herself held the wand.

"You cannot get rid of me," Sybil softly whispered, winding a sunny lock of Lulu's bright hair about her fingers. "Nothing shall drive me away. I will hang on until you love me whether you want me or not. I will have you love me in spite of yourself," and every tone was a caress, every syllable a tender tyranny. And there were so many lovable things about her! Her conversation, rapid, caustic, witty, filled with personal description and anecdote, kept the mind on the *qui vive* to attend, while the ear was soothed by the rare modulations of her trained voice. And intellectually, Lulu did love her, agree with her, appreciate her and delight in association with her. It was but seldom that she was again surprised by a moral lapse—and then, how graceful was the apology. How small and illiberal the moral side of the light sensualism appeared.

Lulu felt but one exaction in all this rosy intercourse. Sybil insisted that she should trust her. "Believe me true, true to the very core, darling. It is all I ask. Look deeper than the surface. Read the core of my heart. In you I see my salvation, my hope of better things. Life has in its way been bitter to me. By some strange mischance, I seem never to have been understood. My quality is so different from the American fiber—yet I recognize in you its counterpart—a quality so subtly deep and rich that the world can never fathom it. Let us fathom each other. Let us prove to ourselves, if to none others, that there can exist between two women a love, holy, pure, exalted, which no change of circumstance can alter, no selfishness or jealousy can make less true. Let us enter into a sweet secret together of undying faith and mutual help, that for once in all this great skeptical world we may bring out the possibilities of womanly character—a loyalty so belied, so scouted, that but to admit it exists is to be scorned." Her flashing eyes and indignant attitude supplemented their eloquence to the appeal.

And remembering with pity the sad tears, the aspiration she had overheard by the sea, her imagination filled with crosses and sorrows which were all the more terrible because so mysterious; Lulu, with all her sweet soul tossed by varied emotions, sprang into Sybil's arms and sealed the compact with a long, clinging kiss, the first that she had voluntarily tendered to her woman-lover.

As time went on the pressure of this exaction began to be felt. Yet so supreme was her loyalty, so self-sacrificing the purity of her intention, that Lulu neither understood nor analyzed her position.

With the enthusiasm of youth which had been so gradually yet surely awakened, she longed to do anything, to give anything, to be anything to show the intensity of her devotion, the unadulteration of her friendship. Fired with the thought that she, in her girlish inexperience, had still in her some magnetic "quality" which held this magnificent woman of the world in the mesh of her lightest will, she abandoned herself mentally and physically to the fascinating pleasure of giving that joy which thrilled the Visonti with visible emotion. Many and many a time when taking their afternoon siesta, Sybil, capturing her hand, had gently drawn it to her own brown throat, her very heart, where, beneath its light pressure, Lulu could feel the blood leap in an ecstasy she could not understand.

"I feel as if I were floating on white clouds, dearest, when you touch me. My body is light as air, and my soul seems to drift into a fairy realm. What magic lies in these precious fingertips to give me such an unknown happiness!" And murmuring sweet poetic phrases, she would entice the pretty hand.

Taking advantage of a sudden influx of visitors, Sybil had begged to be allowed to share her large apartment with Lulu, and although Helen in her thoughtful hospitality had endeavored to leave each guest undisturbed, the assurances of both that it would be only the more agreeable convinced her to arrange it in that way, and soon the two friends were associated far more intimately than before.

And if, with an occasional nod to her original tendencies, Lulu deserted Sybil for a whole day, going away with Guy to spend delicious hours of chat and fun, regaining in his wholesome presence the strong, fresh vitality which was her constitutional condition, she would soon be made to feel how lonely, how sad, how desirous of her Sybil had been. For although Sybil was occupied with her own affairs, she protested that in her heart all was dreariness without the light of Lulu's smile.

Then too, the little demons of vanity and jealousy, which lurk in every heart, were roused by the comparison of Helen's constancy. For Sybil claimed all that was to be claimed from that source.

Lulu was made to feel that Helen was so tender, so generous, so loving, so comprehensive—not like her, cold, sarcastic, indifferent, cruel, irresponsive or careless of the ever-increasing love she had awakened.

That love seemed to close around her, cling to her, fall about her like a beautiful gauze through which she could hear and see the outside world. It was the shimmering film of a soft veil which seemed to shut her in—body and soul—to this enthralling friendship, against which she had but spasmodic inclinations to struggle. After all, having struggled with a vehement, passionate, nerve-shaking revolt, like a sudden fury of anger, suspicion, or unspeakable horror and hate, left her in a weakness, a dullness and indifference, which was only chafed or soothed into passive acceptance again by the soft sarcasms or softer persuasions of her companion.

Of the growing familiarity of this association, Lulu said nothing to Guy, although she daily declared to herself that she would confess—what? That although he had warned her to beware, she had left his desire unheeded? That she had, although he begged her not to stay one moment alone with the Visonti, for several weeks shared her room?

Perhaps that would seem to throw some blame on Helen, and besides, was she in duty bound to run to him with every little thing? Was she not capable of ruling her own affairs, if she could rule this lovely woman with a frown? Her pride, her shame, her sense of the pleasure of her secret, all led her to keep silent, while Sybil had often with pricking pleasantry scorned the idea of masculine intrusion.

"Must we make our lovers our father-confessors, our guardians, our popes infallible?" she cried one day when Lulu said, "I had better ask Guy," about some intended excursion. "Are you at the knee of your future husband, or is he at yours? The attitude of self-abasement would not be pleasing to me, no matter how much I loved a man. And mark me, sweet, what now you offer, after marriage he will exact. But, of course, go, tell him the whole of your dear little heart. Even if you will, tell him of my bondage to you, and let him sneer at what he would call a woman's passion. Subject even the sacred beauty of our love to the cynical criticisms of his man-like analysis. Oh! I am not jealous of him. Do not believe that. I have never intruded myself between you one hair, have I? But, Lulu, my Lulu, do not let him intrude between us," and with a wild, hungry look, pitiful in its seeming intensity, she pleaded as if for an almost lost treasure.

The young girl felt her brain whirl with a sense of her subjugation of this woman. She assumed an expression which infinitely amused Sybil, while it pricked her to sudden wrath. Murmuring her promises and assurances as a mother soothes a nervous child, "Why, dear Sybil," she said, "are you so fearful that my noble Guy could not understand your tenderness for me? You wrong him, I know you do. Should he ever again intimate that he—he—wants me all to himself, I will tell him frankly, that your love and mine is something totally different—so impossible to contain the same elements that are in his love and mine, that they are quite distinct—quite unapproachable by any comparison." And with all the loyalty of her soul aflame, she determined to let nothing so much as cast a shadow over so high and fine a union.

"So he has intimated that I am trying to take you away from him?" said Sybil reproachfully, looking at her as if with a still unsatisfied doubt.

Lulu blushed, remembering his saying about the magnolia.

To hide her confusion, she left the room, flinging her answer gaily back. "Oh, he was a little jealous too."

Sybil grew dark as the cloud-rack that was driving up the sky. As she pushed the blinds wider and felt the first cool drops beat on her up-turned forehead, her stormy brow seemed to invoke the thunder which suddenly rolled across the zenith with tremendous echoes. Casting a long look down the dim hall through which Lulu was passing, she shook with scornful laughter. She tossed her arm lightly towards the retreating figure, and then gazed at its luxurious display of round, soft curves with a sensuous admiration. Tapping the wrist lightly with her fingers and nodding her head towards it gently and slowly, she murmured, "But her young life throbs here."

Medea

CAROL LEONARD

Already my desire and will were rolled—
Even as a wheel that moveth equally—
By the love that moves the sun and the other stars.

DANTE

HANNAH WATCHED absently as the water splashed against the sides of the ferry. The fog was burning off and the sun was beginning to sparkle on the waves. The wind was whipping her hair out of its thick braid and her blue eyes were excited. Hannah grinned as she turned back to her two friends. She was glad they had kept this ritual for the five summers since they had been in college together. Mountain biking around Monhegan Island would be a welcome break from the city's heat and the grind of the advertising agency.

Her friend, Kirsten, was fair with an angelic, chubby face but a wickedly biting sense of humor. She and Kirsten had been lovers for a brief, mostly drunken, period in college. Fortunately, their friendship had survived the fling and they had remained close. Amanda was another story—dark and very striking, although spacey. She was smoking a lot of ganja (and who knew what else) and was becoming increasingly more distant and aloof, sometimes bordering on incoherent. Hannah was a little concerned, but she wouldn't worry about it now. These few days together would be precious.

Hannah was becoming impatient for the ferry trip to be over when she looked down to the first deck and saw a woman leaning against the rail staring out to sea. The woman was tall with slender legs in black leggings and clogs, and a worn suede jacket with the collar turned up against the wind. Her uncombed hair was pulled back and bunched into a ponytail; a brown baseball hat was pulled low over her profile.

Hannah froze. "That's her!"

"That's who?" Kirsten responded

Hannah pointed to the woman. "That's her—the vampira! I've seen that face in my dreams a thousand times. It's her, I'm positive of it!"

Kirsten, only too familiar with her friend's nightmares, muttered, "Jesus Christ, Hannah—for someone who seems so straight, sometimes I think you're more fucked up than all of us put together!"

But Hannah wasn't listening. She was concentrating on the woman below. Hanna draped her lanky frame, posing, against the railing and unleashed her wild mane of copper curls from its braid, letting her hair fly in abandon. Her eyes bored into the woman's back.

The woman turned slowly, looked around, then glanced up. Hannah caught her breath. Yes, that was the face she knew—the face she loved. The woman began to turn back to the rail, then stopped abruptly. She shot her gaze back at Hannah. The woman leaned back against the rail facing Hannah and crossed her arms. Her eyes were hidden behind her sunglasses but her mouth had a definite amused smile. She nodded slightly.

That was enough. Hannah bolted down the steel stairway and boldly approached the woman. The woman greeted her silently with the same bemused look, but behind her sunglasses, she was clearly sizing Hannah up. Up close, the woman was even more beautiful than Hanna had initially thought, although she looked a bit more haggard and ashen. She had a strong jawline and high cheekbones and a laugh line etched deeper on the right side from a slightly crooked smile. Hannah thought the woman appeared to be…what? Early to mid-forties, probably. The woman had an odd silver Celtic cross around her neck.

"I thought vampiras were allergic to silver crosses," Hannah blurted out.

The woman flinched. "That's a strange greeting," she said dryly, turning back to the rail.

Now Hannah felt awkward and suddenly shy. "I'm sorry. It's just that your face looks so familiar to me. You look like pictures I've seen of Elizabeth of Bathory," she lied.

"Ah, yes—the mad vampiress of the Middle Ages. The benefactress nailed by the Catholic Church, as I recall. They claim she had a penchant for bathing in the blood of young virgins, am I right?" The woman waited for a response, then continued, "You seem to know something about these creatures…is this some kind of obsession of yours?"

Hannah stood up straight. She was almost as tall as the woman when she didn't slouch. She faced her squarely.

"Actually, yes—you could call it an obsession, I suppose. But I've been waiting all my life for the vampira to come to me—and I think you are She."

The woman's head snapped back. There was a long silence, then her nostrils flared. The woman leaned her face into Hannah's hair and inhaled her scent deeply. As she drew back, she lowered her sunglasses. Her green eyes glittered far too brightly. She said in a husky whisper, barely audible, "You're bleeding now."

"Yes."

The woman's lips were parted, exposing perfect, strong white teeth. Her breath was shallow and rapid, almost a pant. Her eyes had clouded with desire and the artery in her neck pulsed violently.

Hannah felt her heart beating so loudly it was deafening. Her knees were about to buckle, but she knew she had to complete the dance.

"Yes, I am bleeding now…and I want to straddle your face and bleed into your mouth." Hannah felt suddenly sick from what she had just said.

The woman's eyes flew open. "This is crazy," she murmured, then louder, "Get away from me. I mean it! Get the fuck out of here!" Then she shouted, "Leave me alone!"

Hannah fled and stumbled back up the stairway to her waiting friends. They had heard the woman shouting.

Kirsten looked horrified, "You asshole—what did you do? Totally freak out some middle-aged lady with your sick fantasy? Did you? Hannah, man, you've got to get a grip—this is *not* okay, do you hear me? You're scaring me!"

But Hannah was completely still, a small smile played on her lips, "Oh, no. I was right. That's Her, for sure." A gentle pulsing began in her groin and her scalp started to tingle. She looked back down to the woman who had lit a cigarette and was staring back out to sea.

When the ferry docked and the three women wheeled their bikes onto the landing, Hannah searched, but the woman was nowhere to be seen. They biked for most of the day; the scenery was spectacular. The sun was blinding on the water and the air was fresh and clean. Kirsten and Amanda kept up a constant banter of jibes and bickering but Hannah was uncharacteristically quiet and preoccupied. She was methodically trying to reconstruct the dream that had reoccurred like clockwork since she was a small girl. She was desperately trying to decipher the message in it. The dream was always the same, so lucid, calling to her as though it were another reality. In the dream-time, she was in a circle of standing stones, an ancient place from time primordial. The landscape was as familiar to her as the New England seascape, but she knew it to be in the Western Isles. The place haunted her—the twisted forms of the stones were foreboding, yet they beckoned her. She knew the hulking Callanish stones by heart. In the moonlight she was racing to find the one Beltane stone by the appointed hour. But just as she would approach the monolith she knew to be right, confusion would engulf her, panic would set in and she would race to another. Would she never get it right? The time for meeting was past. She had missed the appointment! She would give in to despair. How could she have been so forgetful? Her movements would still to slow motion. As she stood frozen, her limbs paralyzed, she would glimpse the woman standing in the moonlight with the same look of slight amusement. The woman would approach her and say gently,

"Ah, my love, you are still too young...have patience, we

must wait. We will know when it is time." And then she'd be gone.

Hannah would wake in a cold sweat, with a sense of failure and a feeling that something was irretrievably lost. Her tears after this nightmare were always from a profound emptiness. Remembering the dream now made her feel abandoned, with a deep longing to be fulfilled.

Hannah felt confused and disoriented. She knew she wasn't going to be able to keep the pace Kirsten and Amanda had set. She was even more certain that her mood wasn't going to improve.

"Are you feeling all right?" Kirsten asked.

"Yeah, you're not your usual self," Amanda commented with a concerned look on her face.

"I'll be fine. I'm just not feeling well. Why don't you two go on ahead? I'll meet up with you later."

Hannah biked back to the village. She stopped at the mostly deserted town bar she had noticed earlier. The interior was poorly lit and it took a few minutes for her eyes to adjust to the darkness. At the end of the bar, Hannah saw the familiar figure of the woman sitting by herself. As Hannah approached, this time with a little more trepidation, she saw the woman's face was drawn. She was drinking white wine.

"I thought you'd prefer red wine," Hannah tried to sound cavalier.

The woman glanced at her sideways and said, "Ah, yes, the old imagery of the Queen with a bottle of Claret in her lap—how classic."

Hannah slid onto the barstool next to her, deliberately, casually, brushing her breast against the woman's arm. The woman lit a cigarette. She looked amused when Hannah tried to avoid the smoke wafting her way, but she didn't move.

Hannah commanded her voice to be even and ordered a Rolling Rock. When the bartender placed it in front of her, she drained the bottle. The woman cocked an eyebrow at her and ordered another beer for Hannah and another French Colombard for herself.

Hannah had noticed the strange blue tattooed marks around the woman's right ankle. She felt flushed but braver and said to the woman, "Tell me about those."

The woman regarded her coolly but then her face softened. She nodded and spoke slowly. "My name is Medea. These are the blood marks of my people. When as a young woman I began my first wise-blood, at my menarche rite, I was given the first mark of the waxing crescent moon to honor my crossing the threshold to womanhood. Then, later, when I gave birth for the first time, I was given the full moon mark at the back of my heel to honor my fertility and the initiation into the mysteries of the Mother." She pointed to a blank place, "Later on, I will be marked with the waning crescent on the outside of my ankle when my bleeding time comes to an end." Medea suddenly grinned at her shyly, "It's not time yet, but it's getting closer.

"Now, as for you, Hannah…you're in your fullness right now."

"So, you know that about me?" Hannah was feeling a little irritable and a tad pissed at Medea's assumptions.

Medea continued, "Yes, I could smell you as soon as you entered the building. I was a midwife for many, many years. Somehow I was always drenched in the blood from births and I loved it. I loved everything about birth: the smells, the sounds, the great mystery of life coming back in. I had tremendous respect and awe for the process and for women's power in the moment. Birth blood to me was joyous and sacred."

Hannah pressed further, "Where did you learn of this power?"

The pain flickered across Medea's face. She continued, "My initiatrix was a beautiful red-haired vampira in the Outer Hebrides, in Scotland. She was a midwife as well and I loved her deeply. I thought I was just screwing around—that the power of the blood was just a myth and somehow we were making it all up, some kind of silly girl-bonding thing. I totally ignored the fact that these stories have survived for centuries, that there must have been some basis for their continuation, some truth to it all. Now I know, whenever you awaken these dark rites once held holy, there is a force at work beyond—far beyond—our control." As she ground out her cigarette, Medea's eyes welled-up and her teeth clenched as if to block a flood-tide of grief and memory and loss.

Medea stared straight ahead at the bottles at the back of the bar. "Who knows who was the initiator and who was the victim in it? I don't." She remained motionless, staring vacantly for what seemed like a long time.

When she finally threw her head back and looked at Hannah, it was as if seeing her for the first time. Suddenly, Hannah felt bold, "I want you to show me what she taught you." Medea grinned her beautiful smile.

"So, what brings you to the Blood Rites, little sister?"

Hannah blushed, "My fascination with womancraft began in high school and developed in earnest in college. It was obvious to me that lunar blood was once held sacred. I wanted to know why women's power was deliberately hidden."

"Yes. Lunar blood was the basic ingredient in the Great Rite. Menstruating priestesses of the Goddess would collect their holy blood for the sacrament—the blood of the goddess Charis, Goddess of sexual love. Did you know that the word *eucharist*, meaning communion, comes from the name Charis? In the Old Religion, the Great Mother bade the people to drink of the bloody flow of Her womb, the fountain of life, and they drank in holy communion—*hic est sanguis meus!*—and bathed in it." Hannah was entranced, listening to Medea.

"Medieval priests were right when they claimed that the communion wine drunk by pagans was blood, the original wine of the Holy Grail. Now, the regenerative powers of the wise-blood has become the highest taboo."

Hannah felt completely confident. "You're hungry now, aren't you?"

Medea nodded.

"You want to drink me."

"Yes."

Medea had swiveled on her stool so her legs were parted. Hannah stood between them and pressed herself against Medea. Medea leaned back against the bar. Her hands went up to cup

Hannah's small breasts, her fingers moving to find Hannah's hardening nipples through the fabric of her t-shirt and gently rolled them between her thumbs and forefingers. Hannah felt the warmth shoot down between her legs. She felt dizzy.

Medea whispered, "Are you sure you want this?"

Hannah looked in Medea's eyes and said, "I've been wanting it all of my life."

Medea leaned forward and breathed into Hannah's hair, "I want to fuck the blood out of you."

They took two candles from the bar as they quietly left.

Medea and Hannah traveled in the twilight along an overgrown logging road until they found a pine-needled nest near the lapping tides of the ocean. They sat and looked out over the water.

Medea grinned into the dark. "Salt water has always held such a fascination for me." She lit the two candles and stuck them in the ground.

She wound her hand into the thick mane of Hannah's hair and pulled her to her. Hannah was surprised that Medea's kiss was at first so tentative and sweet, almost awkward. Medea's mouth was closed, then parted as her tongue darted out and ran over Hannah's teeth, tasting. Medea's body relaxed as she let down her guard. The kiss became more fevered, groping, until Medea rammed her tongue into the side of Hannah's mouth and she bit firmly. The bite sent a shock wave between Hannah's legs and she felt a momentary lapse of certainty. Sensing this, Medea became very caring and loving, kissing Hannah's earlobe deliberately, softly, running her mouth down the tendons of her neck until Hannah felt another bite pierce her skin at the clavicle. She felt delirious, but the sensation was too exquisite to object.

Medea pulled back, untied her matted hair and shook it until it fell over her shoulders. She lowered Hannah back onto the pine needles and loomed over her for a moment. In the candlelight, Medea looked like the Goddess herself. Her broad shoulders gleamed. She was narrow-hipped like a man, though her belly was slightly slack from childbearing. She knew she was in her power. Her gaze was direct and she slowly, tortuously, grazed her full breasts over Hannah's, moving down until Medea's mouth tugged on Hannah's nipple. At first she suckled like a baby, playing with it, pulling it deep into the back of her throat. Hannah felt a sudden surge of emotion watching Medea's sweet face at her breast. Then Medea's face hardened and she spat the nipple out to the tip and bit down piercingly. The bite made Hannah throw her head back. "You're not going to kill me are you?" she said, with genuine fear in her voice.

Medea positioned herself face to face with Hannah and said, passionately, "Hannah, why would I do that when I can be with you for as many cycles as you allow? There will be pain for a brief moment but then the pleasure will be so engulfing you will forget...Do you trust me?"

Medea's eyes in the candlelight were so entrancing, so alive and wild, Hannah surrendered the last of her will and sank into the darker mysteries.

Medea watched with calculated certainty and then lightly teased her breasts down Hannah's belly until her mouth was on Hannah's navel. She slipped her tongue into the indentation, then teased and nipped her way to Hannah's springy pubic hair. She stopped to inhale deeply. Yes, blood...that delicious, salty, sweet and musty nectar! The skin of her scalp began to tingle and she let out a low growl. She snaked her tongue down between the silky folds until she circled the nub of Hannah's clit. She drew her head back and breathed her hot breath on it and brushed it with her tongue ever so slightly, teasing. Hannah was squirming with impatience. She reached down and grabbed handfuls of Medea's hair, pushing Medea's face firmly into her. Medea laughed, beginning a more firm and rhythmic stroking with her tongue. Her fingers searching, she spread Hannah's labia and let out a groan when she felt how slick and wet Hannah was. She looked down and saw a trickle of blood coming from Hannah's vagina. Her heart skipped a beat. *Not yet,* she thought.

She slowly, gently inserted her index finger in Hannah and explored around the interior walls. She felt for her cervix and tentatively checked the os. It was rigid and closed. "Damn,"

Medea thought. Hannah was rocking her pelvis against Medea's tongue. Medea stroked with two fingers that exquisitely sensitive swelling in the upper anterior wall. Hannah was whimpering, pleading, "My god, what are you doing to me?" Medea increased the pressure and her motions became more rapid. Hannah was opening to her now, so Medea used three fingers to stretch her gently. Three, then four, then all to the knuckles. She felt Hannah tighten and contract momentarily, so she waited until Hannah's muscles relaxed. Hannah was moaning softly and rolling her head from side to side. She opened completely to Medea then, and Medea's entire hand entered her past her wrist. Medea cupped her fingers and swept around and down the entire billowing cavern. Hannah felt an indescribable power surge through her and felt as though Medea was searching, grasping for her very soul. She let out a loud, low groan and Medea became more aggressive. She was getting very aroused herself. Hannah began ramming down on Medea's hand with urgent thrusts, crying, "Fuck me, Medea, fuck me harder!" Medea balled her hand into a fist and pounded into the cul-de-sac. Hannah's fingers clawed the earth, grabbing fistfuls of pine needles. She was so close to coming.

Medea quickly drew back and felt for the outer cervical os—now very open and receptive—and Medea easily inserted her finger up the cervical canal to her knuckle. She reached the unyielding, rigid internal os—the last gateway to the inner sanctum, the Holy of Holies, the cauldron of all humankind. Hannah's sounds were still low and Medea glanced up to see the whites of Hannah's eyes rolled back. Medea's breathing was ragged as she positioned her finger at the final portal. Medea prayed, "Please, Dark Mother, make this fast."

She gathered up all her unnatural strength and with a violent thrust, she ripped through.

Hannah's shrill scream pierced the still forest night.

Waves. Waves of ecstasy flooded over Hannah as she felt her blood gushing out of her as Medea drank. She could hear Medea moaning now as her body made involuntary, convulsive movements. Medea reached a hand up and pressed down hard on Hannah's belly to express the last of the blood from her uterus. Medea was shaking, finally sated. She then brought her attention back to Hannah's clit and sweetly, gently sucked on it until Hannah came with tears of relief and release.

Medea rested her head in Hannah's pubic hair, kissing the inside of her thigh until Hannah's breathing slowed to normal. Hannah reached down and cupped Medea's head to pull her to her. When Medea raised over her, she saw in the candlelight a terrifying, wild animal—Medea's mouth and chin were dripping with Hannah's bright red blood; clots of blood were sticking in Medea's matted hair. Medea kissed her lovingly and Hannah tasted the sticky, sweet taste of herself.

Medea positioned her pelvis on Hannah's hard, muscled thigh and began a slow rocking motion increasing in tempo. She was gazing directly into Hannah's eyes and her eyes growing wider and wilder as she began to come. Her nostrils flared and she bared her teeth. All expression left her eyes and she arched her back as the spasms racked her body. She let out a hoarse howl and collapsed on top of Hannah, burying her face in Hannah's hair.

"Oh, Hannah, you sweet, sweet girl." Her voice was filled with gratitude.

They lay silently entwined in each other's arms for a long time. They drifted off to sleep listening to the harsh calls of night herons.

Hannah woke to the early morning sun warming her naked body. She felt a profound sense of well-being and fulfillment. *Medea!* She turned and sighed with contentment seeing Medea sleeping soundly next to her in the dappling sunlight. She was sleeping on her back and Hannah studied her face closely. Now Medea's skin looked radiant and glowing, all traces of exhaustion literally gone. She looked so vulnerable, sleeping slack-jawed, Hannah couldn't resist touching her face to trace that beloved profile. Medea opened her eyes and smiled.

She reached over and softly stroked the copper curls framing Hannah's face. She raised up on one elbow to examine Hannah more carefully. She definitely looked paler, even her freckles seemed faded. She had dark circles under her eyes, but she looked healthy enough and positively happy. She checked the color of Hannah's fingernail beds and she knew she'd be fine in just a matter of days.

"Hannah, I really want to thank you with all my heart for being brave and trusting me. I needed for you to feed me last night. I guess I could say I owe you my life. The blood is an incredible gift, a beautiful blessing from Her. I needed to be reminded of that. Thank you, sweet girlfriend."

"And now...?"

She cupped Hannah's chin in her hand and kissed her on the forehead. "I'll come to you for as long as you can tolerate it...and I'll be eternally grateful to you. But for now, I have to go."

"No!" Hannah gasped, "You can't! You can't leave me now...I love you, Medea!"

Medea sighed, "You must not be with me except in your next moon cycle. There is no other way. Believe me when I say there is too much sorrow in it. I'm sorry."

As Medea turned to put on her clothes, Hannah was surprised to get a very clear whiff of her scent. Amazed because just yesterday, Medea had smelled like fresh rain. Now her smell was pungent, filling Hannah's nostrils, clouding her brain. Hormones! It then became obvious to her that Medea herself would be bleeding in just a day or two....

Medea turned and caught her breath. Hannah's eyes were glittering far too brightly.

Femme-de-Siècle

Lawrence Schimel

for Lesléa Newman

SHE WAS cruising me something fierce. The way only a femme can do it; she ignored me. Not even a stray glance in my direction, and that was how I knew I had her. She was paying attention to my every move, watching me like a hawk from beneath those long dark lashes in order to pretend not to be noticing me.

I walked into a corner to think and instinctively tugged on my baseball cap's brim, pressing it down against the back of my neck as I wondered what to do. I stopped myself. I knew she knew I was fidgeting, even though she was looking the other way. She was watching the bulldagger at the other end of the bar, but it was all just to make me jealous. My eyes kept coming back to her. She was gorgeous: Geena Davis come down to earth—and flirting with me! That pale skin, all that wavy hair, those lips: so full, so ripe, aching to be kissed. I was so hot I knew I must be leaving puddles on the wooden floor. But, damn! I didn't know how to approach her.

Fate gave me an opening. She reached into her purse and drew out a gold cigarette case. I grabbed the lighter in my jacket pocket and tried to think of what to say. "Can I offer you a light?" sounded too corny. "Give you a light?" "Let me light up your life...." I kept my mouth shut. I walked over to her and lit the end of her cigarette. She took a long drag from the thin, unfiltered cigarette and held it for almost a minute while she stared, unflinching, directly into my eyes until I felt like I was flying, swimming in the warm, dark essence of her soul. Then she blew a perfect smoke ring, which ghosted above my head like a halo.

Her voice was liquid music when she said, "Thank you."

That was the beginning. She came home with me that night, and every night that week. I was in heaven. She wasn't the kind of femme who liked to just lie there during sex; her sex drive was something else. She would strip me out of my clothes in no time flat the moment we walked through the door.

I never really learned much about her life away from me. I tried to ask gentle questions without seeming like I was prying, but she never really opened up when she answered. It was only natural that I would be curious about her—hell, I was totally infatuated with her—and I tried to encourage her by talking about my life and past with her. I've always loved long, gossipy pillow talk sessions after sex, but she was as silent as a statue: beautiful, pale, and pretending to be asleep. I mean, there's trying-to-maintain-an-air-of-mystery, but there's also trying-to-hide-something. She always came over to my place—I didn't even know where she lived beyond a general section of town—and it was always sex right away and late into the night and straight to bed. I began to wonder if our relationship was actually so hot, or if we were having such desperate sex in order to not give me the chance to notice something. Not that I minded the sex, of course, but I began to pay closer attention to her. And that was when I noticed that she didn't eat.

We'd been seeing each other every day for a week and we'd never had a meal together. She would nibble at stuff, but she didn't really eat anything. After sex, besides loving pillow talk, I get the munchies bad, especially when we'd been going at it for a long time. She would take the tiniest bites of what I tried to feed her, smaller than dainty—crumbs, really. And that was it.

I decided to test my theory when she came over the next evening. I asked her—before she had the chance to tumble me into bed or on the couch, or in the hallway, or atop the kitchen table—if she wanted to split a turkey sandwich from the deli around the corner. I told her I was famished and needed to have something right away.

"I just ate."

"Why didn't you wait for me?" I cried. I was hurt. But I also felt a sadness for her deep inside of me as she answered that she had held out for as long as she could. I didn't want her to waste away did I? She was incredibly thin, it's true, but not all bones and skin: she was still sexy and curvaceous. But I was also sure she was anorexic.

I didn't know how to approach her about it. I rubbed the back of my neck as I lay in bed, watching the gentle curve of her spine as she "slept" post-coital before me. I wished I had left my baseball cap close enough that I could reach out and put it on without having to actually get up and hunt for it. Our life together was rushing ahead on a stream of inertia, and I was afraid that any change or confrontation would disrupt it completely. She would continue hurtling forward with her life as fast as ever, but in a different direction, away from me. I didn't want that to happen so I held my peace, biding my time and watching her even more closely when it came to food.

And then it wasn't just the food. Two nights in a row she got up while I was sleeping, and left. Not a word of explanation—just put on her clothes and slipped out. I pretended not to notice, but I couldn't help feeling betrayed. We'd been dating for three weeks and already she was having an affair! I didn't understand it; it wasn't as if the sex wasn't satisfying her. I was attentive to her and always pushed her limits just a little to keep things fresh; I always asked her what she wanted, what turned her on.

"I'm always very moody when I get my period," she told me the next night. We fucked for hours. But still she got up in the middle of the night and slipped out of the house. I hadn't been able to sleep, anxiously worrying if, or when, she would get up and leave me. I, too, threw on my clothes to follow her. The night was quiet and clear; a harvest moon sat fat on the rooftops, about to slip out of sight. She was single-minded in her journey, not bothering even to look about her as she made a beeline for Primrose, which was open until 3:30 AM on Saturdays. Although I felt betrayal like a cold knife stabbing my stomach, I couldn't help thinking it was foolish for a woman to be out on her own at this time of night, even in this quiet neighborhood. To be so careless about her personal safety—it was inviting trouble.

I didn't have the heart to follow her into Primrose and confront her. I waited down the street, feeling like a gumshoe as I stood in the shadow of a doorway. She didn't leave me waiting long, the bitch! Five minutes later she came out trailing behind this insignificant wispy stick-figure of a woman. I'd been fantasizing about her and that bulldagger doing the hot and heavy, but this was all wrong. I didn't know what she saw in her tryst-trick, and that wasn't just jealousy talking! The woman looked unhealthy, pasty-white in the moonlight as she and my lover hurried arm-in-arm towards one of their apartments. I wondered if I would finally learn where my mysterious girlfriend lived as I followed them, every moment wanting to run up to them and stop them. I didn't know which one of them I wanted to hurt more; I was ready to pummel both of them. Was this the same woman she'd been seeing these last few days, I wondered, as they slipped into a brownstone. They'd certainly picked each other up quickly enough, as if it had been prearranged.

The lights in a second floor window went on. Mad with jealousy, I raced down the street, looking for some way around to the back of the building. An alleyway led toward the gardens that ran behind the buildings. There was a wire fence, and I didn't think twice before beginning to climb over it. I froze as two garbage cans shifted against one another, but no one seemed to notice the racket.

I moved from garden to garden more easily now, jumping fences when there weren't gates. Sure enough, I found the apartment where the two of them were reflected, *in flagrante,* shadows against the drawn window shade. I'd recognize that hair anywhere, the silhouette of those breasts as her shirt was pulled over her head. How could she do this to me? I watched her lean forward and kiss another woman's lips, nuzzle greedily at her chin, her neck. I turned away and climbed over a fence and threw up. I don't know how I got home, but I woke up on the kitchen floor, missing her and hating her and not knowing what to do about anything.

I cried when she showed up that evening like nothing had happened. *Me.* Bawling like a baby because she'd been unfaithful.

"I'm not cheating on you," she insisted.

Was anything she had told me true? Or had it all been lies and secrets: the anorexia, those other lovers, what little she had told me about her past….

"I *saw* you!"

"And what did you see?"

How pert your breasts were as you took your shirt off, how eagerly you leaned into her embrace. I was speechless.

"What you saw is… is that…"

I couldn't stand the pussyfooting around. "Just say it. You're fucking another woman."

"…that I am a vampire."

I burst out laughing. I couldn't help it, I'd been crying for so long. It was just so preposterous.

She didn't find it funny. "It's true," she said. She smiled at me, wide and toothy, and my blood froze. I blinked to clear the tears from my eyes and stared at her fangs that looked like something out of a bad movie. She closed her mouth.

"I'm not cheating on you."

I didn't know what to say now, what to believe. Or how to feel about her. Was my girlfriend even human?

"Just assuming for the moment that I believe you, which I'm not sure I do, why three nights in a row? Just how much blood do you need to drink?"

"It's because of my period. I always need extra, this time of the month."

There were more plausible alibis for her to have chosen, if she'd wanted to just put me off. I wanted to believe she wouldn't lie to me.

"It's not an easy thing to tell someone. It's like coming out all over again. Coming out of the coffin."

She came over and sat next to me. I was uncomfortable when she touched me, in part because I was so attracted to her as she lifted my head to look at her, then leaned forward to kiss me. These lips, I thought, have drunk blood. I thought I'd have been repulsed by the idea, but I was suddenly wet. Her kiss was gentle, full of meaning.

"I think I like you a lot, too," she said, understanding—really understanding—why I'd been crying. What was I going to do with her? Not just sexy, but caring, too. So what if she was a vampire? I'd dated girls who were into kinkier things.

I wiped my face with my sleeve and smiled at her. "It must be hot. They must have a mondo hickey when they wake up the next morning."

We laughed, falling against each other so comfortably. She held me, wrapping her arms about my shoulders and resting my head against her belly, just cradling me. I had been lost in daydreams the moment I saw her: my hands running across her thighs, the taste of the pink aureoles of her breasts, her hair spilling around my face as she slid her body along mine.... We were pulling at each other's clothes. Pure and mutual desire, making love as a communion of spirit and passion, a cleansing of misunderstanding.

She nibbled at my breasts, working her way towards my collarbone in tiny bites, and I bared my neck for her, trusting.

She stopped, pulling back from me.

"Why only femmes?" I asked her, finally opening the dialogue between us. "You don't like the idea of having sex with your food before you eat it? There are some girls who get into that, y'know? Wild sex and then a nice salad; cucumbers, carrots, zucchini...."

She laughed, and bent forward to lick my belly. "Femmes are more likely to be anemic."

This time it was me, holding her away, so I could look at her. *"What?"*

She ignored the way my voice had jumped an octave and tongued the crook of my elbow.

"Less calories. I'm on a diet."

I couldn't help myself; I nearly fell off the sofa I was laughing so hard.

"What's so funny? It takes work to keep this figure, you know." She slid her body against mine, reminding me how much I enjoyed her figure.

"I knew it all along. Only I had it backwards. I was positive you were anorexic because you never ate food. Now you tell me you're a vampire, so that explains why you don't eat. But it turns out you're still anorexic!"

This time it was me who, after a long few minutes of silence, gently lifted her face to look at me. "It doesn't hurt them when you take blood does it? I mean, maybe it hurts a little, but it won't kill them, right?"

She shook her head, hair spilling about her like a cloud of midnight.

"Next month, I want you to take blood from me when you need it. Promise me you will."

"I promise."

I rolled her over on the couch, looking down at her beautiful body, before leaning forward to devour her. "Good."

Holding her, after sex, she didn't pretend to be asleep right away. I whispered in her ear, "I can't wait for it to be that time of the month."

She didn't answer me, not in words; she just kissed me, and held me tight.

The Tale of Christina

Cecilia Tan

I KNOW A SECRET *as old as the world, a secret as deep as the ocean and as dark as coal. I know how vampires are born. I also know what you are thinking right now: you think of the bite, the blood. But it is not blood that makes a vampire. No. It is the* wanting. *Vampires are forged in the heat of desperate desire; vampires are birthed in the waters of a need so intense that their very souls do drown. Have you ever wanted something so much? So much that you would die for it? Kill for it? Lose your soul for it? So it is with vampires. When the wanting becomes of fever pitch, the magic ignites and transforms one from mortal being into the pure embodiment of hunger, of need, of desire. Ah, but you want to know, what about the blood? You are so sure it must have something to do with that.... Well, perhaps there is magic in all blood ties. Of course, the wanting hurts. It hurts more than ever. And the blood...the blood is only one way to quench the fire. Perhaps the quickest, easiest way, if just for a little while. I have discovered others. What else will you ask? Holy water, the sign of the cross...I have not found them deadly. But the Christians have good reason to call us enemies, for their faith is founded on denying one's desires, delaying one's gratification. For us, that is our life. We live for desire eternally.*

I thought I might say something like that to Christina, if the time was ever right for it. She would be thrilled by the dramatic flourish, the poetic turns of phrase. I passed the time imagining my delivery of such a speech and the circumstances under which it would come. I looked at my silver pocket watch—she was late for our second date. With measured steps I paced the tiles of cracked marble in the vestibule of her building and resisted the urge to ring her buzzer again. If she had been there, I would have known. That is one thing about the magic. Want something badly enough and you know where it is. I wanted Christina. Tonight I thought I might have her.

Our first date had been a chance meeting a week ago; I'd gone out to a new club to see what there was to be seen. It satisfied my sense of irony to go to what was billed as a "vampire theme night." For some time now I'd become aware of a fashion called goth, a mixing of all the sublimated fears and beliefs of an earlier age with the trappings and trimmings of the same: white lace, red roses and black hearts. Shelley's and Stoker's misunderstood monsters—icons for these young ones—melded with more modern demons: industrial, postmodern, cynical. Dear, dear children… they realize that Hell is this Earth, and allow themselves to exult in it. When all life is pain, from the pain must come joy.

In one of the myriad bookstores in Cambridge, I had found homemade magazines filled with their dark poetry, blurred photocopies of musicians they idolized, letters and essays and more, all revealing their essence to me. That is where I'd found the flyer inviting me to enter their world—held one night a week—vampire theme night. I looked forward to seeing these new children, to see if they were everything I hoped they would be.

I paid the cover charge and entered the place. A few heads turned as I stepped into the main room. I had gone back to the clothes I liked best for the occasion: an off-white lace cravat, black waistcoat, silver cufflinks…accoutrements which had suited me so well in the past century. Only at vampire theme night could I wear such things without seeming out of place. I noted a few others about in ruffled shirts and fine brocade; still others were in black leather, or neck to ankle in black satin. My eye was more than pleased to note that there was one—and then another, and another—whose gender was obscured by light, by makeup, by mannerism. I might find prey here, I thought. But even better, I might find kin.

The room pulsated with want. I tasted loneliness, alienation, isolation. There was the tang of lust, especially from the dance floor, and the sharp spice of a sudden, mad desire from a white-haired girl seized with the urge to kill herself, which then faded when a black-maned boy (I think) took her by the hand and led her out of my sight. It was then that I caught sight of her, of Christina, carrying a bouquet of black silk flowers and wearing what could have been a wedding dress if it hadn't been night black. Her hair, which was flamingo pink, seemed too bright for her monochromatic demeanor. She settled herself at a small table by the dance floor, a few friends shedding their leather jackets around her as they went to join the others gyrating and swaying to the beat of the music.

I did not approach her. I took up a spot at the bar and asked for ice water, amusing myself by watching the androgynes sliding from posture to posture. The music was heavy and moving, like a Gregorian chant set to a rhythm. In fact, I think that is exactly what it was. In my time, it was much easier for a woman to pass as a man, because no woman would be seen with such short cropped hair, in trousers, and smoking. Now, women did these things with such regularity that it would not twist anyone's perception to see a woman in trousers. Now it has turned to the men to put on makeup, heels, maybe a dress to cross the barrier. Here the point did not seem to be to pass as a member of the opposite sex, but rather to seek a maddeningly erotic mixture, to disguise whatever gender one had while at the same time radiating a unique kind of sexual allure. I found it heady and encouraging, a touch of fishnet or velvet here, lipstick or eyeliner there.

Yet of them all, the one I wanted was Christina. Christina, so dearly femme, clutching her funereal bouquet.

Eventually I had gone near her, near enough to taste the want coming from her—the taste of something she wanted so dearly that it was buried deep inside, under layers and layers of affectations and peer pressures so dense I couldn't sense it clearly. Yet I wanted her. I wanted her, and I sat there wanting her until it worked the magic so that she came to me. And I did what any civilized person would do. I took her out for coffee.

She agreed to meet me again, to go out for dinner at my

expense and to go again to the club, this time arm in arm. And yet, where was she? I rang her buzzer again, just in case. Maybe she was in the shower, but no one answered. No, I would have known if she was there. My connection to her was strong. I sat down on the cracked marble steps to wait.

Our coffee that night had been dark and rich and just a bit bitter, like the taste of her soul as she told me about her parents and her sorry adolescence. She was not as young as I had first thought. Regardless of how many years she had lived, there was still a great deal of that confusion that infects the young, a search for who she was and who she wanted to be.

It was a pain I had never understood very well. I had always known what I wanted to be, had always striven for it, despite the fact that it would always be unattainable. I hadn't listened to my parents' guidance, or even my society's disapproval. And I told her this.

The next word caught in her throat and I thought I had it—I thought I knew what she wanted, what she wanted to be. Something hidden under her fear, a spark of wanting something outside of the mundane. Something with a taste of the forbidden. A lesbian. A woman's woman. And yet she wanted to remain the frail flower she was. It did not match her picture of lesbianism, but I thought her perfect for it. What she wanted was a woman's love, and that was one thing I could give her. I wanted her so much that I could no longer taste the coffee at all. Perhaps the Christians and I do have something in common after all—I, too, delay my gratification. I spoke to her of the future that awaited us and made the date for dinner with her.

But where was she? I looked at my watch again. Something must have gone wrong. I thought again of how her wrist bent as she reached to pick up her ragged bouquet, of how her fingers had slid off mine as she slipped into the cab, of the delicate curve of her collarbone above the satin trim of her dress...and I let the wanting take me. The wanting poured from me in invisible waves, seeking her.

It was some minutes before I sensed her—to the north, probably across the river, in the direction of the club. I couldn't just hail a cab and then tell him to drive "thataway." I set out, my head pounding as I made my way from the brownstones and trees that lined her street toward the boulevard.

I told you the wanting hurts. It always has, but it becomes bearable after so many years. I had awakened the wanting in me, and it would have to be slaked soon, even if just for a little while. *When you find her,* I thought to myself, *she will be mad with desire for you.* I knew of two ways besides the blood to quench the wanting: to satisfy someone else's want was one way; to exhaust oneself with the friction and fusion of sex was another. With Christina, perhaps I would have both and sleep soundly for many nights to come. The anticipation made my head pound all the more.

A man on a bicycle whizzed past me, then came to an abrupt stop at the corner; a sudden ragged sob tore loose from him. Homesickness descended upon him. I shook my head, trying to contain the wanting, to reel it in. I had been careless. In his proximity to me he'd caught a whiff of it. He wiped his eyes on his sleeve, shaking his head in puzzlement, and went on his way. I hugged myself as if that might help to keep the wanting in and focused myself on her and her alone.

By the time I was halfway across the bridge, I could sense Christina more clearly. She was nearby. I came to a neighborhood full of three decker houses and postage stamp yards. She was here, in one of these houses.

I stopped in front of a house that had once been painted blue, showing underneath a flaking beige that had been hastily or lazily applied. The only decoration was a hand written "For Rent" sign in the front window. But there were lights on in the upstairs apartment, and it was there that I sensed her.

A few seconds passed and the aroma of her changed. And then I heard her scream.

I tried the door, found it open, and took the stairs two at a time. The door to the second floor apartment was locked, but old and flimsy. The hasp gave way on my second push. I found myself in a kitchen and homing in on the eastern corner of the house—a bedroom heavy with the scent of cheap incense. At first

I wasn't sure if that's really what the scent was, or if it was the stink of the man I was facing when I pushed open the bedroom door. A man who wanted things I did not want to know about. He was naked and his black hair hung around his eyes like weeds.

"Who are you?" he asked; in his hand was a knife stained with that unmistakable red. All I could think was what an irrelevant question...of course I was the one here to stop him. I didn't answer. Instead, I walked past him to where Christina lay crumpled upon the bed, her shock of pink hair hiding her face. I tried to take her in my arms, but she pushed me away without looking up.

"Hey, I'm talking to you." I looked back to see him licking the knife. "You her mother or something?"

"My name is Jillian," I said, hoping that Christina would recognize my voice. He was running the knife blade along the outside of his arm, drawing long, thin lines in his flesh. Now it was my turn to ask the stupid question.

"What are you doing?"

"Aw," he said, "I wasn't going to hurt her." I could smell the rotten stench of a lie coming off him. It was his own blood on the knife. If I had arrived later, it would not have been—of this, I was sure. I wanted to take her out of here, away from him. Seeing her curled up, naked and defenseless, had made the want a screaming nightmare in my head.

"Christina, honey, are you all right?" She was crying. I turned to pick her up, as if I could carry her, unclothed, to safety.

He gave himself away. I turned to face him—not because of the electric change in him—but because he muttered, "Bitch," as he lunged at me with the knife.

The knife sank deep into me, in the hollow between my right shoulder and collarbone. His eyes were still on the hilt of the knife when I took him by the throat. Now I had pain beyond pain. The magic shrieked the damage to my perfect shell, and this idiot was bleeding from several places where he had cut himself. He was gasping as I pulled him to me to lick at the wounds he had inflicted upon himself. But there was only a trickle, and a river was pouring out of me.

"Christina..." I said, my voice a deep rasp, "pull out the knife." I could not do it and hold on to him at the same time. "Please...." She was on her feet, a sheet wrapped over her shoulders, her eyes wide. She reached a hand toward the hilt. He flailed a bit and she pulled back. I tightened my grip on him. "He can't hurt you." She grasped the hilt with one hand and it slid out of me, slick and wet and dark. But her eyes never left my face. I forced out the words, "Turn away." I knew she wouldn't—she was pulled into the vortex of the wanting, the magic. The wanting coursed through me, and it seemed his neck came to my mouth of its own accord.

I drank until he was dead. It had been a long, long time since I had done that. I had taken blood before, but the wanting was so severe that I needed to drink deeper and deeper until the blackness of his death ran through me, too. My own death was one thing that I could not have. I drank until we both fell back upon the bed like lovers, his fingers pushing feebly at me as he slipped away to whatever afterlife there might be. I lay back, a heaviness in my limbs making it hard to do anything else.

I saw Christina still standing there, as she had been through the whole feeding, the knife in her hands and the sheet held tight around her like a shroud. Perhaps I would be giving my vampire speech sooner than I had planned. She looked for a moment like she wanted to say something. As the words came to her lips, tears came to her eyes, and she began to sway. I stood up to catch her as she fell sobbing into my arms, and the knife fell to the floor.

My speech didn't go the way I thought it would. There was no other explanation for what she had seen. The knife wound was completely healed by the time we returned to her apartment. She had seen me exhibit a strength that was unhuman. Not to mention that I drank him dry. Now that I was full, my senses were dulled and I had to listen with care to what she said or risk missing the nuance of what she really meant. She had turned to me as soon as the door to her sanctuary, a small studio with an alcove hung with black curtains, was closed.

"You're a vampire," she said, as breathless as if we'd just run up the stairs instead of riding the elevator. Her eyes were not narrowed in accusation but wide with wonder.

"Yes."

She faltered a bit as she lowered herself onto the bed. In a long black t-shirt and jeans, she seemed more frail than she had in lace and satin. Her eyes seemed far away and her lips trembled. I knelt by her feet and took her hand.

"It's all right. I'm here. He's gone." She looked at her little white hand in mine and mustered half a smile from her overworked lip.

"I didn't know he would be like that," she said. "I'd seen him once before, at the club. And when I ran into him today and he asked me…."

When she didn't go on after a moment I asked, in the gentlest voice I had, "What did he do?" She shook her head, whether to remember or forget I don't know, and squeezed my hand harder.

"With the knife, he wanted to…it was too much…." She pressed her legs together. I didn't need to hear any more. He'd lured her with the promise of sex and given her violence. I held her against my breast and rocked her like the child she was inside. And when she broke away, she kissed me like the woman she was.

I know there was still the taste of blood on my lips, but she didn't seem to care. Even though my senses were still deadened from satiation, every nerve in my body told me of her need. I remembered my original plan for the evening, to make love with her, to give her what she wanted. She welcomed me into her bed. I shed my bloody clothes and luxuriated in the feel of skin against skin.

"You're so soft," she remarked. *Let her enjoy it,* I thought. *At least someone will.* Her fingers slid over the place where the knife had been in me and she sighed a deep, luscious breath. I took my time with her; as I came to touch or kiss each unexplored patch of flesh, I gave her a moment to follow with me in assent. Her shoulder, the hollow of her bosom, the soft skin beneath her navel. While my tongue was searching at the parting between her legs, as I listened to her sigh and moan, the wanting began to seep back into me. I prayed to myself, *Let it not be as strong this time.* But I could already sense the oldest, most familiar tingle in it, the feeling I had tried to suppress all these years. Christina was alive in my mouth now, with frantic jerks and cries. I wanted to reach out with my senses and find out how much more she wanted, but I didn't dare let the wanting loose—not when memories and old, old desires were beginning to brim up. Not now...*why now?* I could keep it in check. I kept my mind on the task at hand, licking her, tasting her salt. She held on to my short hair and kept me in place as her pleasure rose up and she rubbed herself against me. *Christina, my sweet, my dear one....* When at last she went limp, I stopped and pulled back to look at her.

She was looking up at me with dreamy eyes and smiling. Yet I realized her wanting was still there, and it was beginning to rage back stronger than ever in me. Wasn't she sated? She seemed to be waiting for something. She put her arms around my neck and whispered into my ear "Take me...." I pushed her away, reeling from the deepest stab of the wanting that I knew.

"I can't." Wasn't that obvious? How could she taunt me so, when she could see my body.... Perhaps I was simply doomed to live out this wanting again and again. Isn't that what it is to be a vampire? To embody the want that made me this way?

I cursed myself for a fool. She wanted something I could not give her, something this woman's body would never have, even though I will walk the earth for eternity wanting it. I pulled back from Christina then, as if she were too hot to touch. She seemed to be transforming into Selene before my very eyes.... Selene, the lover I had kept as well as I could in my mortal life, with my hunting rifles and my hounds, my trousers and pipe. We could have married, I think, and no one would have thought it odd or out of place because at that time no one knew I was a woman...except her. And it grew to grate on her. She hated me in the end, when, drunk with passion, she had insisted over and over, "Take me, take me!" and I couldn't. Not the way she wanted. Not the way I wanted. I was consumed with frustration and desire. I was consumed with the wanting. She shoved me aside and told me that she had been sleeping with one of my stablehands, that I would never satisfy her. I flew into a jealous rage and she fled, never to return to that cursed life. Neither, I thought, would I.

I took up one of my hunting knives and thought to end my miserable sham of a life. I slashed my wrists and knelt by the fire thinking on and on how unfair it was.... I had lived as a man, succeeded as a man, but I could never be a man. My mind whirled from the sex, the pain, the violence. When the magic began to take me I did not recognize it for what it was. The surging of fire through me—perhaps that was what dying felt like. But then I saw the cuts healing. I felt my consciousness expanding....

And here I was with Christina, not Selene. She held me by the hands and said, "Please...." There was none of the cruelty in the tone that had made Selene's voice so cutting. She pulled me down onto the bed again, and nuzzled against me. This is not Selene, I reminded myself, and I tried to look into Christina's eyes. Finally, in confusion and desperation, I let my senses out again, reaching deep into her now, and found her defenses gone. She was completely ready to bare her hidden desire to me.

"Make me a vampire," she whispered. I held her for long moments as I let that sink in. Her desire for the forbidden, to step outside society. Her poor judgment about the blood fetishist turned rapist. Her wonder, joyous wonder, at my performance with him. The idolization of my kind by these children, who already knew that life was about wanting and about pain. And now, as the primal wanting coursed through me anew, I realized I would find no relief from it here. Because I could not give her what she wanted. If I had a way to make her a vampire, it would quench her desire to become one. Without the burning of an unfulfillable desire, she could not cross over.

The pain seemed to hiss through my chest and into my head as I took a deep breath, so tempted to take the quick, easy way out of the mess I had created. But killing her was not something I wanted to do.

"I can't," I said again, as she tried to show her neck to me.

"But...?"

"Shhh." I held her head against me again. She was so small, so beautiful. So young. She would outgrow this fascination, wouldn't she? No, probably not—having met me, seen me, living with the knowledge that she now had. I had known other mortals in my years who had known the truth, but none who had sought to join us, knowing what it was to exist only to live unrequited forever. I thought of the others I had seen at the club. They were, in their own way, all vampires.

That is what I told her. I tried to explain the essence of the wanting, the pain of an unfulfillable desire that consumes one body and soul. She cried clear-eyed tears of revelation, as if I had spoken a truth she had always known but never voiced. She did not believe in God or Heaven, but she believed in me and my kind, and she believed in the pain of living. Her faith I had affirmed.

We are all accursed to walk this earth with our unfulfilled desires, both you and I. And when you walk the path to your desire, my friend, may your walk be a short one, as short as mine is long.

Orphans

THOMAS S. ROCHE

THE CORRIDORS ramble on endlessly, miles of a black velvet, candlelit nightmare. My Vibram-soled Docs pad on the hardwood floor. The beat of the music churns inside my breastbone, rising and falling, changing in timbre and song as I wander from one area of the club to another. I cross dance floor after dance floor illuminated by black light and liberally dusted with black-clad clubgoers.

Waves of incense smoke trail through my hair, seducing my senses with its sweet perfume. Gothgirls wander past me, holding each other in the darkness. Wraithboys sporting white face paint and black lipstick caress each others' bodies in the shadows of the small rooms off the corridor. I seem to be going in a big circle—every time I turn a corner, I am afraid I'll find Catherine standing in front of me. I realize that my tears have spoiled my makeup—a kind of goth fashion statement, I suppose. Even the knowledge that I've reached the pinnacle of postmodern fashion doesn't lessen my despair.

Skinny Puppy fades into Nosferatu fades into Sisters as I wander the endless corridors, searching for escape or solace. I catch a bit of a Fade to Black song, then the gentle caress of Siouxsie's voice, and then Diamanda's wail. I think I recognize Pavarotti's voice. My father was into opera—the most fucked up music possible. Strange thing to play at a goth club....

I lean up against the wall, completely disoriented, and try to get my bearings. It doesn't seem possible that the place could be this huge. How can I be so hopelessly lost? There can't be more than three or four dance floors in here...can there?

Two girls, identical twins wearing identical dresses of black lace, wander by carrying small tins of chrism. They've paused before me. I stand motionless as first one, and then the other, anoints my forehead. Each one kisses my hand before they wander off.

I slump against the wall. My head is spinning. I feel a surge of regret at what happened between Catherine and myself, the argument we had on the dance floor. Thinking about it only makes me cry again. I sink to the ground, letting the tears flow. *Catherine, oh sweet Catherine... you've gone to Hell, girl, and you're taking me with you.*

The swell of Pavarotti's voice caresses my ears.

We came to the Orphanage seeking solace, a safe place where Catherine and I wouldn't be constantly going at each other like we were in the apartment. Catherine is so far gone, I can barely talk to her. She's no longer the Catherine I loved—the Catherine I still love.

The hearing beat the hell out of her.

She misses Alexander; she mourns for him daily. Her parents won't even talk to her about seeing him. They've stolen him from her with the power of the courts—the inquisitors. Catherine's quit drugs and is in therapy, but Alexander is still gone, maybe forever. Her skin has become the color of ash, her hair as brittle as straw. Her eyes have become bloodshot and her lips drawn and blue-gray. Catherine, my lover, is a walking corpse.

It just hurts too fucking much to think about it. I ask myself for the thousandth time, how can her parents do that to her? The courts ruled in favor of them in part because of Catherine's previous drug use, but more I think, because of me—because she was living with a woman. They call it "practicing." Actually, we've gotten pretty good at it. And that was a problem for the judge.

When the men in black suits came and took Alexander, wrapped in his blue blanket and clutching his Elmo doll, Catherine didn't even cry. She just stood there on the curb, her mouth slightly open like she was trying to remember what she was supposed to say. Three weeks later, in the middle of the night, her soul died.

She and I never speak to each other anymore unless we're bitching at each other. And we haven't made love since the hearing.

I, too, am dying. Living with Catherine is killing me. The blood has been drained from my flesh. The life is being drawn from my soul, the last sparks smothered in the weight of Catherine's despair. I have to move out. Of course, I'm broke and in debt, still trying to pay off the semester of art school with the meager earnings from my shit job at the head shop. Every once in a while I think of moving back in with my parents, but that's before I remember that they threw me out. My parents have convinced themselves that they don't have a daughter. Somehow that's less painful than having a daughter who is going to burn in Hell.

I stand up, looking around me. I'm not sure where I am...lost in the Orphanage. I stumble into one of the rooms off the main corridor, only to find myself in complete darkness. The door has vanished behind me. Reaching for where it should be, I trip and find myself on my knees, a pain shooting through my wrist where I landed.

I no longer hear Pavarotti. Now there are female voices, not coming from the speakers; the clarity is overwhelming. I feel myself slump to the ground.

Far away, in what seems like a nightmare, a slow goth bassline, somehow soothing, begins to play beneath the voices. I hear someone very close to me...smell a dark, musky, female smell. An arm slides around my back, another under my thighs. I am being lifted. I'm back in my father's arms—he used to carry me up to bed after I'd fallen asleep on the couch watching old Vincent Price movies on TV with my mother and him. I even recall the smell of him...but this smell is different, a feminine smell with the same enormous, comforting bulk.

Whoever it is lays me on a bed and begins to take off my shoes.

This dream is so delicious I don't want to spoil it by moving. I do, however, open my eyes. Nothing. The room is pitch black. This has to be one of the rooms that the Orphanage has had fitted with beds as a symbol of decadence—but those rooms all have lit candles in them and are without doors. There are no lights in this room, and there is most certainly a door.

I hear a voice above me, feminine and soothing, singing an aimless lullaby above the bassline. I feel fingertips on the buttons of my shirt. I sit up, suddenly afraid.

"Who are you?"

"Be still," comes the reply. I have to obey the warm, familiar voice and those gentle yet firm words. "You've made your way to the Orphanage. Now we must see if you can find your way back."

I remain silent, still as in death, as the cold fingers remove my clothing.

I lay nude on the silken bedcover. I feel warm, sleepy and comfortable. I can smell a gentle, coppery scent in the air, but I can't bring myself to move for fear of disrupting this pleasant hallucination—the first pleasant experience I've had since Alexander was taken away.

Although my eyes should have adjusted by now, I still can't see.

I feel a hand on my belly, drawing slowly up my body. I can feel warmth, softness, the gentle touch of breath against my ear as a woman speaks to me.

"My name is Lamia," she whispers. "Your lover's soul came to me when it died. Through miles of black corridors and the ache of your despair, you have found me. Do not worry. Alexander will be returned to her." She touches my forehead where the gothgirls had placed the scented chrism. "You have been anointed for me. You have been baptized with blood and pain. Come to me."

The music stopped long ago.

As she kisses me, her serpent's tongue is slipping into me, seducing my soul, devouring my need, extinguishing my pain. I sense light around me—candles are being lit one by one. Lamia kisses me deeper; her hands find my hair as she snuggles on top of me. I am encompassed in her warmth, held down by her weight. Her tongue traces a path down my body, across my breasts then to my belly. I know instinctively she is going to feed....

I look down. I see drops of blood scattered across my breast. My tongue is bleeding. I feel a curious wave of regret and terror, but I am alive again as Lamia's mouth finds my cunt. I stretch, tangling in the silken sheets, looking around desperately: crowded around the bed, but keeping a respectful distance, are dozens, perhaps hundreds, of gaunt, white-faced women in swirling black velvet forming a sea of spectators. I am clawing at the silken bedcover when Lamia's face appears above mine.

"Drink," she tells me, closing my eyes with her fingertips. The weight of her body comes down on me as she presses her bloodied lips against mine. The taste is strange, yet somehow familiar. I have tasted it somewhere before, in a dream or in a nightmare. I am aware after a time that I am feeding on blood from Lamia's tongue, blood which is dripping from her tongue into my mouth. I feel a wave of terror and shame; an agonizing pain seizes my stomach.

Lamia pulls away, wiping her mouth just above my head. I am staring up at her, seeing her clearly for the first time. I recognize the face as if it were the face of my totem. "Mother of God."

"She's not here," says Lamia, slyly, as she lays a white fingertip across my lips. "I am."

I am still in agony—I am gasping, squirming for air. I feel as if I've eaten something horrible. But there is a curiously pleasant ache to my body as well, as after hours of lovemaking or exercise. I double over as Lamia slips off the bed. She disappears into the crowd of velvet-clad women.

The agony has subsided. I begin to tremble in fear, and I am suddenly cold. Dozens of nearly identical white faces, black-lipped and hungry, are gazing down at me as they close in around the bed. They are going to do as Lamia has bade them.

I whimper as they descend on me, their mouths sucking me all over. Enveloped by an infinite pillow of black velvet, I feel their smell surround me, choke me until it swallows my fear and I begin to drink the delicious aroma deep into my soul.

I don't know how long I've been lying here on this bed of velvet and silk, enveloped by vampires. I don't know if I've died, though it seems that, despite the fear, I've gone to heaven. I memorize the texture of black velvet, the sensation of fingertips on my face. They're leaving me—the vampire women in their black velvet are, one by one, flying away like bats into the darkness.

Lamia kneels by the bed, taking my hand in hers. She kisses my lips, no doubt tasting traces of her own blood. She places her warm, slick lips next to my ear and whispers softly to me.

"There is one here whose lips you recognize."

I nod. It takes all of my effort to move my head. I am covered in tiny, sensuous bites, from which the vampires have drunk their fill. I draw my eyes across the crowd of women, seeking...seeking until I find her face.

I hold her in my gaze, desperate to feel her once again, to taste her once more. She slowly steps out of the group.

"You know her," says Lamia.

"I think so."

"One never knows for sure, does she?"

Her face is white, ashen, an image of death. It reminds me of when she used to wear whiteface, years ago. The death mask she wears of late is that of a different caste. The curve of her lips, the beauty of her tortured eyes, the descent of her throat into that black velvet collar—it is all so achingly familiar.

Lamia beckons. "Come, Catherine. Your lover is among us. It is time for you to leave the Orphanage. Marian must bear a gift to the land of the living."

Catherine is upon the bed. She is presenting her throat to Lamia, who is taking it hungrily. I close my eyes as they lean over me, warm droplets falling into my mouth. Now Catherine is upon me, feeding me. I suck greedily once I taste her and begin to drink.

I recognize the taste. I know it well. It is the taste of walking Alexander to the park, of putting him in the swing, of buying him an ice cream cone at the corner store run by the Russian family. It is the taste of eating dinner at the Mission—Thai food—just the two of us, our love seasoning the curries and the milky iced teas. It is the taste of the autumn breeze liberating us as we walk up the street to Muddy Waters to get cappuccino. It is the taste of our bedroom, the smell of our love on a Sunday afternoon, our bodies sprawled on the soggy futon, sunlight slanting across Catherine's belly as I kiss her and hold her like I will never let her go.

Catherine is gone suddenly, her black velvet gown left lying across my body. The candles begin to go out, one by one, in a circle around the room. The wraiths disappear into the darkness, and Lamia kisses me one last time, licking the last of Catherine's blood from my lips.

"Bear your gift well," she tells me as she slips off the bed. "Keep it close to your heart and protect it with your life. Bring it to your lover—she is very much in need."

I am wandering, wandering, swirling in black velvet through the endless maze of corridors. This time my footsteps are sure. This time I know my way. A gothboy, singing "Gimme Shelter," and his drag queen boyfriend drift beside me. The wraithgirls appear in front of me and wipe the chrism from my forehead with a sandalwood-scented handkerchief. Two familiar shapes are in a corner performing an obscure goth ritual with an ankh and a plastic skull.

Catherine appears like a ghost-vision, filling the corridor with her scent—her dark, musky scent; her bright, coppery scent. *I come bearing your soul, sweet Catherine. Drink.*

She watches me approach. I read the look on her tortured face. She isn't angry that I disappeared for so long. She isn't pissed off about what I said earlier. She just wants me back. I put my arms around her.

"I thought you weren't coming back," she says to me. Her flesh is still ashen. I nuzzle her throat, feeling her warmth against my face.

"I know baby, but I've got something for you. Everything's going to be all right."

A bassline, like a soothing old friend after midnight. Fade to black.

Cinnamon Roses

RENEE M. CHARLES

I DON'T KNOW if it's because people buy so heavily into the mythos of vampirism (y'know, the gal/guy-in-a-sweeping-cape-swooping-down-on-her/his-prey's lily-white, blue-veined throat batcrap), or if it's because they have this idea that we vampires just need a suck of blood every day or so to keep body and soul in one just slightly undead package, but being a twentieth-century working vampire is *not* just a matter of staking out a little patch of earth under an abandoned warehouse somewhere out in the hinterlands of the city—c'mon, get real.

Spending twelve or more hours a night biting and swooping and not much else is fucking *boring.* And it doesn't contribute squat toward the rent or utilities on my basement apartment in Greenwich Village, either.

Besides, just because a gal gets a little more than she bargained for during an admittedly dumb unsafest-sex-of-all fling with some guy she met in some club she can't even remember the name of (oh, I made him wear a condom, but that didn't protect my neck...) it doesn't mean that she suddenly becomes the reincarnation of Dracula's bride. I still needed to make a living, and since I'd been a hairstylist before...well, you've got to admit, scissors and razors do have a way of occasionally drawing blood.

And from personal experience, I know that vampire bites feel a heck of a lot like the touch of a styptic pencil...down to the not-quite-needle-sharp tip pressing down on warm flesh.

Getting my boss to let me change my hours from mid-afternoon to evening to predawn wasn't difficult; the place where I work, the Heads-or-Tails, is one of those places that specializes in punk, S/M, adventuresome types—full body waxes, razor and lather shaves, even a little extra stuff on the side (regular customers only—cop shops can't afford to send in decoys week after week)—so it isn't unusual to see just about every type of person coming in for that special cut or shave at any hour of the night.

And at a hundred bucks a pop and up, the Heads-or-Tails never closes. So when one of the stylists demands a change in working hours *right now*, the management is more than happy to oblige, especially when she (as in me) keeps drawing repeat nocturnal customers....

Another misconception about us vampires is that if we keep on doing what we do best—a.k.a. neck-biting and blood-sucking—eventually we'll infect the entire fucking world, because our victims will infect victims of their own and so on, until you're looking at one of those Andy Warhol's *Dracula* situations (the whiny vampire strapping his coffin on top of the touring car and motoring off in search of fresh "wurgin" blood). Get off it, do you think that one sip from a person is enough to make them go mirror invisible (which is another load of bullsheet—sorry, but the laws of physics don't work that way, though it makes for a nice special effect in the movies, I'll admit!) and start draining the family dog for a pre-bedtime snack? I had to spend a week with my nightclub Nosferatu before sunlight began to make my skin itch, but I can still put on my lipstick in the mirror, thank you!

So, a slip of the disposable razor here, or a nick with the scissors there, and it's good-bye hunger, but not necessarily hello fellow nightwalker. Not unless *I'm* interested in some continuing companionship over the course of a month or so. And even then, I make certain I know the potential victim well enough to be sure that she or he will be in a position to tap into a private food supply without attracting attention. C'mon, do you think those ER nurses on the graveyard shift keep missing your veins by accident? Or those dental technicians can't clean your teeth without drawing blood?

But sometimes, no matter how much a gal exercises caution

and forethought, not to mention common sense, there will come the day when that certain customer walks in, and every vein in her body, every blood-seeks-blood-filled throbbing vein, cries out to her brain, her lips, her cunt: *Take this one...don't ask any questions, don't think about the night after...just take this one.*

(Doesn't even matter if *this one* is a gal or a guy; skin touching skin is gratification enough, and fingers and tongues more than equal a prick...there's nerve endings enough to go around all over the body.)

For me, the first sign that a customer is a *taker* is her smell: clean, healthy blood surging through her veins just a few millimeters under the unbroken flesh—for each of us, the name, the associative taste, we give to that good blood-odor differs. For me, it's cinnamon; cinnamon that's been freshly scraped from the stick, that raw, so sharp-it-tweaks-your-nostrils tang, so fresh and unseasoned, the smell soon becomes a palatable taste even before the first drop caresses my tongue.

(How else do you think vampires avoid HIV and AIDS? Once you've had a whiff of that moldy-grapes and stale-bread odor—naturally, this perception differs from vampire to vampire—you can smell a victim coming at you from two blocks away. Three, if the wind is blowing past them.)

Oh, all non-infected normals smell somewhat like cinnamon to me now; as long as you're reasonably healthy, the cinnamon-tang is there. In most people...well, it's more like a cautious sprinkle of the spice over toast, or across the top of an unsealed apple pie. Maybe it's all the *stuff* people take; additives, drugs, you name it. But in a taker, that fragrance is a living part of her, like an extra finger or breast. Richer and more lingering than the smell of sex, more piquant than ejaculation seeping out of your crevices.

But the blood isn't the whole reason for that desire to own, to make a normal into a new-blood kin, even though it is the most tangible reason; for me (at least), there has to be a certain look in her eyes, a vulnerability that goes deeper than mere submission. A look that says, *What I am now is not all I could be.* Doesn't matter if the look comes from the eyes of a straight or gay or female or male body, either. Like I said before, there are nerve ends aplenty all over the body. Age isn't a biggie either, although most of the clientele of the H-or-T are youngish, adventuresome.

Color, background, whatever—none of those things matter either. Maybe because we vampires live so much in ourselves, and are ruled by what runs through our bodies and not over our bodies, that which is within others speaks to us so eloquently, so desperately.

Even if they themselves do not realize that inner need....

Despite the air conditioning in my private cubicle (set on seventy-two degrees instead of something cooler—newly shorn flesh, especially a large area of it, does tend to chill easily) the muggy heat of the late July night managed to seep into my work space that particular evening; I was just about to slip off my panties and position myself directly in front of the unit for a few moments when that smell hit my nostrils. *Taker coming.* I quickly lowered my suede skirt and smoothed down the short-cropped hair, which covered my head like a sleek skullcap, before glancing about my work space to make sure everything was in perfect, customer-ready order: Unopened bags of flexible-blade razors—check. Cleaned and oiled clippers, trimmers, edgers—check. Shave creams, mug soaps, depilatories—check. Thin rubber gloves—not that I really needed them, but Health Department regulations are regulations—check. Hot wax—check.

By this time, I could hear footsteps coming closer down the narrow tile hallway between workstations. *This one's a woman,* my brain told my body. My labia began to do a jerking, twitching dance against the already damp fabric of my panties, but I made my other set of lips form themselves into that slightly vacant, blandly professional smile all of my customers get when they part the thick curtains separating my cubicle from all the others in the H-or-T salon.

In deference to the heat outside, she was wearing a halter top, shorts, and slip-on cotton-topped shoes, the kind the Chinese make by the thousands in an hour or so. Can't rightly say I remember what color any of her clothes were; but *her* colors...well, you know how it is when you see your first really brilliant sunrise, don't you? (Even though those are forbidden to my kind, the memories—the skills and the need to go on surviving—remain.)

Within, she was a molten cinnamon, and without, she was a sunrise, or a sunset...whichever is the most vivid, the most full of heartache. Russet hair flecked with streaks of natural gold and near-orange fell across her forehead and shoulders, like lava arrested by a sudden chill, while her eyebrows were twin arching bird wings above eyes, green like gumdrops and suck-it-'till-your-mouth-puckers hard candies, or new leaves in the sunlight-I-could-no-longer-see green. And she had the type of skin that let that cinnamon-scraped-from-the-stick lifeblood of hers shine through in delicate vine-looping trails of the palest filtered-blue and labia-pink. Real redhead skin. And I don't know why it is, but so many true redheads like her are so naturally thin, not to the point of bones sticking out, but covered with just enough flesh. Breasts small enough to cup in a woman's palm, but the nipples would be big and hard enough to make an imprint on that same smallish palm.

It was painful not to be able to drink her in for as long as I wished; but staring at the customers, especially new ones (and most especially takers) can sometimes send them turning on their heels and diving through those heavy curtains, never to be seen or smelled again. Fortunately for me, she was nervous enough not to notice that I was staring at, no... *devouring* her. Her green-beyond-green eyes were timidly lowered, darting to a picture she held in her left hand, then back at a point right around my waistline. She probably didn't even realize I was doing the looking.

Which suited me just fine.

I could see the picture she was holding; a newspaper clipping of that one model, the French-Canadian one with the dragon tattooed on her shorn scalp. Well, at least it wasn't Susan Powter; I'd have been loathe to try and bleach that exquisite liquid cinnamon hair of hers.

"Uhm, the woman up front said you do...what'd she call it? 'Full head shaves?' "

Customer or not, taker or not, when she said that I felt a sharp pang not at all unlike the first time my lounge-lizard Lothario sank his incisors into my neck. Even if it meant being so close to her exposed neck, shearing off that mane wouldn't give me the usual pleasure I felt as my labia quivered in time with the buzzing hum of the heavy-duty clippers which would send my hand and arm quivering as I'd take off the longest layer of hair. Usually, shearing off hair could be a sensual, aesthetic experience above and beyond the sight of those subcutaneous veins resting in the flesh of the newly exposed neck; the way it rippled as it fell away from the scalp, drifting down in feathery piles to the floor, sometimes thick swaths of it touching my bare legs on the way down, tickling like a man's hairy leg brushing against my own, or the way the light picked up the sheen of untanned, milky skin under the quarter-inch stubble, and as the lather was swept away by each pull of the blade, the play of diffuse light on naked flesh and the silky feel of it through the thin rubber gloves were usually enough to give me an orgasm on the spot.

Then again, most of my customers had average, unremarkable hair. Being obvious about my potential pleasure would've driven her away before I'd come even within tasting distance of her exposed flesh and spice-laden veins, so I smiled more naturally and replied, "That's my specialty...I can do either lather shaves, or just clipper—"

Somewhat reluctantly, the taker replied, "No, not just clippered...my boyfriend, he has this thing about skin, y'know...all over."

The words "my boyfriend" were an explanation—and a challenge. Most of my female customers went for the Powter or O'Conner look because their lovers were spending too much time ogling those chrome-plated, unattainable TV visions, and judging by how few of them returned for touch-ups, either their boyfriends took over the daily shaving chore, or they realized that wearing a wig on the job was a consummate drag (the salon also sold wigs on the side), and went back to doing the hair-spread-over-the-pillow thing, and to hell with what Boyfriend thought. But there was always the possibility that Boyfriend might like an entirely naked girl, too, so as casually as possible, I assured her, "I'll do a close job, so your boyfriend should be pleased...you said 'all over', didn't you? As in—"

At that she blushed; the rush of blood coming to her cheeks made my mouth water and my labia jerk so hard I had to (albeit casually) cross my legs as I leaned back against the counter top behind me. Reaching up to toy with a thick curl of hair for what might be the last time in a long time—depending on how pleased Boyfriend was with my efforts—she licked her lips and said softly, "I was embarrassed to ask out front, but I figured since there's the word 'Tails' in the name of the shop...he'd like it...y'know, down there, too. He said he'd like to be able to—" at this she blushed deeper, until the reddish glow seeped into her makeup-free eyelids, " 'see the rose as he's plucking it.' I know it sounds weird, but...well, he's given me a lot of flowers, on my birthday and on our anniversary of when we met and all, all of them these pink bud roses...and what he has the florists write on the cards can be a little, y'know, embarrassing, especially when they deliver the flowers to the bank where I work, but...you know. It's not like it's real cool to send a guy a rose in a bud vase...."

Her words took me back to my first few nights with the one who took *me* into this world, the same world I was aching to bring her into with a few styptic-stinging kisses. I'd been spread open before him on his bed, a pillow placed beneath my behind, and he'd been tracing the contours of my glistening pinkness with a lazy forefinger, telling me, "Do you ever look at yourself, opened like this, in a mirror? I thought so...have you noticed, how each lip curls just so, like the petals of a bluish rose, until they meet in a tight cluster right...here?" With that, he rubbed my clitoris in a feathery, semicircular motion with one finger, while using the other nail-down to trace a thin jagged line from my navel to my slit, which became a reddish inkless tattoo for a few seconds against my growing-ever-paler skin. "See how you'd look if you were a rose? 'Rose is a rose is a rose is a rose?'" he asked, indicating the carmine "stem" he'd drawn upon my flesh.

I'd had to arc my neck at a slightly painful angle (mainly it made those tiny incisions there hurt) to see his handiwork, and even then all I had the power to do was moan a soft assent before the full force of the orgasm swept me away into a crimson, eye-lids-closed private world....

One slightly deeper whiff of this woman's scent told me that Boyfriend couldn't be my old sanguinary sweetheart—all vampires have a special, very indefinable sweetness, like old chocolate in their blood—but I felt a certain kinship to him anyhow...even though he would soon be my rival.

Poor man...I can understand why you would want to see all of her, touch and taste and caress it all...even if you're willing to forgo the ripple of hair under your hands, or the moistening mat of curls surrounding that soon-to-be-plucked rose....

A little too much time had gone by while I was bathing in the sweet come-like stickiness of my memories; the girl's face became slightly anxious, and she asked timidly, "I know it *does* sound silly...I mean about the rose—but could you do it?"

Not letting the sigh I felt escape my lips (although I couldn't resist the urge to lick them), I replied, "Of course, would you mind slipping out of your shorts and panties? It'll just take me a couple of minutes to get ready."

While the young woman slowly unzipped her shorts, her face wearing the expression of a thirteen-year-old reluctantly disrobing for the first time in gym class, I prepared the small rolling table with the clippers, five-pack of razors, shaving foam and scissors. Then, as she wiggled out of her shorts to expose her pale green, lace-trimmed cotton briefs (I could make out the plastered-down arabesques of russet curls over her mons), I placed a long fresh towel over the seat of the barber's chair in readiness for her. As she watched me pat the white towel down on the leather seat, she gulped, but stuck her thumbs down into the lacy waistband and—with her heart pounding so hard it made her left breast quiver infinitesimally—pulled down her panties, then gracefully stepped out of them. With a schoolgirl-like neatness, she bent down, knees together, picked up the briefs and shorts, and placed them on the stool where I usually sit between customers.

She must really care about her boyfriend to put herself through this...I only wonder if he'll be so grateful once I get through with her, I asked myself as she sat down primly on the barber's chair, legs tight together, and arms gingerly placed on the padded armrests. Barely able to suppress a smile, I picked up a drape, put it around her neck (the sensation of her hair sliding over the tops of my hands as I secured the Velcro tab behind her long, thin neck was like silk rubbing against my most sensitive parts), then said, "You'll have to open up...I can't do a full job otherwise."

For a second she just sat there, looking at her draped body and exposed, tousled head for a moment in the numerous mirrors surrounding the chair, a shocked expression on her face...until she caught on, and obediently parted her legs, so that the drape tented over them above her spread thighs. The funny part was that she had the drape hanging over her snatch....

Before I picked up the clippers, I gently gathered the hem of the drape in my hand and pulled it upward, until the extra fabric was bunched in her lap. Across the room, she was reflected in all of her waving, curling, sunset-varied hues, with the deep pink rosebud center of her right in her line of vision; from her sharp intake of breath, I realized that she'd never seen herself so open...or so vulnerable.

"It won't...y'know, pull, when you cut it...will it? Going against the grain—"

"You'll be surprised how good it can feel," I assured her, before asking the standard question at the Heads-or-Tails salon. "Which do you want done first, heads or—"

"Uhm...I never thought about...maybe my bottom...no, wait, better do the head," she finished reluctantly; most women go that route, even though it seems illogical. I suppose it has to do with the thought of someone touching the private parts...especially when no woman has done so in such intimate circumstances before.

And like most first-timers, she kept her eyes closed once I switched on the clippers. Usually, shearing takes about ten or fifteen minutes, if you're careful, and feel for any unexpected bumps or irregularities on the skull. But doing this one, this taker, took a full twenty minutes. With each slow, cautious movement of the clippers, another drift of sun-kissed hair filtered down, caressing my shins before it rested on the floor at my feet. The reddish stubble still caught the light well; from certain angles it resembled the nap on velvet, with a pearl-like white base.

And this close to her scalp, her bare neck, the odor of fresh spicy cinnamon was overpowering, achingly intense...but I knew I'd have to wait for my chance to savor her. Clippers seldom cause nicks serious enough for a stinging kiss....

Once the last of that rippling, gorgeous hair was liberated from her scalp, I tilted the chair backwards, so that her head rested on the sink drain, and—after warning her what I was going to do—ran warm water over her scalp, prior to lathering her up. By now she was beginning to relax; a thin smile even played on her lips. But she still wouldn't open her eyes, not until I'd massaged her wet scalp for a few seconds, and she fluttered her eyes open before asking "Is the cream heated? My boyfriend, he does that before he shaves—"

"Naturally." By now, I was shaking so much inside I was afraid I might cut her for real, but once I picked up the can of heated cream and sprayed a dollop of it onto my left palm before smoothing it onto her scalp in a thin layer (too much lather and you can't see the grain of the hair—and shaving against it can be painful—but too little, and the razor pulls), my pre-vampire days hairstylist's auto-pilot took over. Once she'd been fully lathered, the foam barely covering the velvety bristles of her remaining hair, I washed off my hands, then pulled on the fresh pair of rubber gloves necessary before I could pick up one of the new razors from my little table. Even before I'd gone permanently nocturnal, I'd been the smoothest shaver at the salon; the trick is applying just the barest amount of pressure against the gently rounded surface.

And this time, when she closed her eyes, it was purely in

ecstasy; the heightened rhythm of her breathing was unmistakable, even under the clinging drape. Whether or not a female customer I was shaving was an intended meal or not, I loved to see that blissful look on their eyes-closed faces as the gently bending steel caressed and cleaned their scalps; I suppose it's the look men strive for on the faces of women they're fucking—that away-from-it-all gratified expression.

As I worked, I was so taken with stealing glances at her face in the surrounding mirrors, in fact, that her head was smooth and pearl-like before I'd had a chance to inflict a deliberate, albeit minor dripping wound. Her eyes were still closed, so I debated whether or not to run the razor across her delicately veined white flesh once again, as if seeking stray hairs, but it would've spoiled the moment, somehow. It was my fault. I'd missed my first chance at her; going back to correct my omission would be too cruel—

She's just a taker, not anything that special to you, I sternly reminded myself as I lowered the chair for a second time, to wash off the last bits of cream from her head, prior to lathering it up with an aloe-based shampoo. That she'd moan when I worked the foamy lather around her smooth, moist skin was a given...but what wasn't so much of a given was the way that low, purring moan would make me reflexively arch my pelvis, the muscles in my inner thighs twitching in time to her barely voiced cries.

That was when I realized that her heretofore unnamed boyfriend was definitely going to get more than he'd bargained for when he sent her here. After all, roses and pearls are equally beautiful to more than one beholder....

Once I'd toweled her off, and then slathered a fine coating of the most delicately-scented oil I could find on my counter onto her shorn pate (I didn't want to risk obscuring that heady cinnamon bouquet which all but radiated from her newly bare skin, like shimmers of heat coming off a smooth road in the summer sun), she timidly reached up to run a smooth hand over her satin-fine skin...then gave me an unexpectedly wicked grin, her eyes twinkling.

"I didn't think it'd feel like this," she whispered throatily, her breasts rising and sinking deliciously beneath the drape, "I'm glad I left the best for last...."

That a customer got into the whole bareness thing wasn't unusual, but the transformation from schoolgirl shy and demure to completely relaxed and ready for more in this particular customer-cum-taker was enough to make my heart lop so crazily I was afraid that it would stop from the extraordinary effort. It was only then that I glanced down at her waiting quim; the image of roses after the rain, when the sunlight (a still poignant, missed memory for me) hits the petals, revealing the subtle blend of colors on each one came to mind...and this time, the scent of that brown, powdery spice, mixed with her own rose oils, was all but intoxicating. I had to steel myself against simply going down on her then and there, and tearing into that delicate wrinkled flesh with incisors bared openly.

Now my problem would be restraining myself; it would never do to drink too deeply, especially from such a nest of tender folds and hidden creases, lest her boyfriend (*and my enemy,* I decided) notice my handiwork too soon before she left him.

That she would eventually leave him would now be a given; for a brief moment I wondered if *my* vampire master, he of the no-name nightspot so many years ago, had known that I'd end up leaving my previous boyfriend, as he looked and spelled and wanted me so very deeply, with a yearning beyond reason, even beyond basic desire. (Once, he'd told me that my "scent of dark coffee" was like a syrup cascading down his throat....)

But still, her boyfriend had been so intuitive to her potential shorn beauty, and so eager to witness that naked splendor, that this act of taking would haunt me...even as it fulfilled me in a way no palm pumping mere *man* could fully understand.

Putting on my best, most professional face (at least for the moment), I switched on the smaller set of clippers and let my hand be guided by the individual mounds and deep valleys of her flesh; once I asked her to spread her legs out wider (I'd already lowered her chair to a reclining position, the better to see her curl-hidden petals), but apart from that, neither of us spoke—nor had need to. Clipping the mound of Venus is trickier than clipping the scalp; the area is tighter, and more springy under the clippers, but this time around, gathering up my concentration was an almost super nonhuman effort.

Freed of the damp ringlets and tufts of russet hair, her mound was a mottled pink-white (from the pressure of my fingers as I spread the flesh to accommodate the clippers), but when I applied a small disposable makeup sponge (sea sponge; it has a rougher, more French-tickler-like texture) dripping with warm water to her stubbled flesh, it soon turned an even, conch-shell pink. I couldn't resist pulling aside her inner labia, to expose the glistening slick skin within to the light, and was rewarded with a subtle upward thrust of her pelvis. That she was enjoying this gratified me, almost as much as taking a sip of her blood...*almost.*

The lathering was dreamlike in its slowness; up, down, and around the tender, sweet-scented flesh (by now, her own unique scent formed a heady counterpoint to her blood-bouquet) until the patch of foamy white was fully covered up to the tips of the stubble. Taking up the first of two fresh razors (sharpness is essential...and not just for my own vampiric purposes), I freed her flesh from the coating of foam stubble and drying foam, until she was almost entirely naked, more naked than she'd been at birth, in all likelihood...save for a last tuft of hair I'd left untouched, close to the gently rounded spot where the tip of the mount meets the tuck of the flesh hiding her clitoris.

True, that tight curve was the most difficult place to shave, but that wasn't why I left it for last. Unless I became as animal-like as the bat most non-vampires erroneously think we can turn into at will, I'd have to be cautious now...lest my actions become too obvious, too potentially frightening....

"Could you be very still now? This is the trickiest part. Otherwise, I might nick you." Getting the words out without bending down and biting and sucking and drinking her in was difficult, but she didn't seem to notice that anything was out of the ordinary.

As she spread herself even wider, so that the last daub of nearly dried foam covering that dime-sized patch of remaining hair was almost perfectly level before me, I had to release some of the pent-up desire in me...if not my thirsting desire, then my sexual wanting.

Using both hands, I gently fanned my fingers over her taut lower belly, her tight thighs, not letting myself touch her exposed petal-softness, her intricate folds and crevices of glistening flesh, until I was sure that my hands wouldn't shake too much. I only needed a tiny nick, not a bloodbath...even though I would have loved to have felt her cinnamon warmth coursing over me in hot, spurting runnels....

Taking up the second of two razors I'd used on her, I let the sharp steel bite ever so superficially into her pale skin on the downstroke. I don't even think she felt the nick, it was so slight, but my mouth flooded with burning saliva when I saw the tiny dark pearl of blood rise up in all its spicy-warm splendor.

"Uh, oh, I drew a bit of...lemme get the pencil," I mumbled, before grabbing the styptic wand off the little table...and then clutching it so tightly in my fingers that it bent out of shape as I knelt down and ran my tongue over the welling beads of ruby sustenance, before my incisors bore down on the pliant, perfumed flesh of her outer labia, her mons, her inner thigh....

For a moment, a deeply shamed, yet animalistically exalted moment, I felt a stab of fear-pleasure—here I was, being so obvious, so greedy, and with an uninitiated taker. But in the next moment, as I stopped my inhalation-like feeding, I realized that she was moving her pelvis and hips in time with my movements, my feasting on her very inner essence.

Sated enough to stop what I was doing, I guiltily wiped my bloody lips clean with the back of one hand (then licked said hand with a fly-flick of my tongue), before standing up between her still-splayed out legs, and letting my gaze meet her own. Reaching down with her right hand, she gently touched the place where I'd been sucking out her blood, gave me a smile, one that reached up to those memory-of-sunlit-leaves green eyes of hers, and then said softly, "I suppose I can tell my boyfriend that even my rose had some thorns…" before beckoning me back to sup once more on the glistening feast between her outspread legs.

But the best part of what she said was the way she made "boyfriend" sound so casual, like something ultimately fungible after all….

Later, without needing to ask, she simply agreed to come to the salon on a thrice-weekly schedule, for "more of what you did tonight." I didn't ask her name; eventually, she became Rose for me, and that was all either of us needed. But that first night, as she dressed and covered her pearlescent scalp with a scarf she'd brought along in her shorts pocket, I busied myself with a little gift—a token of future losses, actually—for her soon to be ex-boyfriend.

It's funny, but if you take those pink and red colored specialty condoms (like I said, the Heads-or-Tails offered occasional "extras") and after opening the packages—twist and bunch them just so, then attach them with plastic-covered twist ties (green ones, naturally—we keep them on hand for securing garbage bags full of clippings) to those wooden sticks we use to stir hair dye, they look an awful lot like rosebuds.

Maybe her boyfriend did find my gesture touching (Rose never felt the need to say, later), but from my point of view—not knowing how faithful he might be—I was only protecting my investment against blood that stank of moldy grapes and bread long-gone stale.

The Bloody Countess

ALEJANDRA PIZARNIK

Translated by Alberto Manguel

The criminal does not make beauty;
he himself is the authentic beauty.

JEAN-PAUL SARTRE

THERE IS A book by Valentine Penrose which documents the life of a real and unusual character: the Countess Bathory, murderer of more than six hundred young girls. The Countess Bathory's sexual perversion and her madness are so obvious that Valentine Penrose disregards them and concentrates instead on the convulsive beauty of the character.

It is not easy to show this sort of beauty. Valentine Penrose, however, succeeded because she played admirably with the aesthetic value of the lugubrious story. She inscribes the underground kingdom of Erzebet Bathory within the walls of her torture chamber, and the chamber within her medieval castle. Here the sinister beauty of nocturnal creatures is summed up in this silent lady of legendary paleness, mad eyes, and hair the sumptuous color of ravens.

A well-known philosopher includes cries in the category of silence—cries, moans and curses form "a silent substance." The substance of this underworld is evil. Sitting on her throne, the countess watches the tortures and listens to the cries. Her old and horrible maids are wordless figures that bring in fire, knives, needles and irons; they torture the girls, and later bury them. With their iron and knives, these two old women are themselves the instruments of a possession. This dark ceremony has a single silent spectator.

I. The Iron Maiden

...among red laughter of glistening lips and
monstrous gestures of mechanical women.
RENE DAUMAL

There was once in Nuremberg a famous automaton known as the Iron Maiden. The Countess Bathory bought a copy for her torture chamber in Csejthe Castle. This clockwork doll is the size and color of a human creature. Naked, painted, covered in jewels, with blond hair that reaches down to the ground, it has a mechanical device that allows it to curve its lips into a smile, and to move its eyes.

The Countess, sitting on her throne, watches.

For the maiden to spring into action, it is necessary to touch some of the precious stones in its necklace. It responds immediately with horrible creaking sounds and very slowly lifts its white arms which close in a perfect embrace around whatever happens to be next to it—in this case, a girl. The automaton holds her in its arms so that it is impossible to uncouple the living body from the body of iron, both equally beautiful. Suddenly the painted breasts of the Iron Maiden open, and five daggers appear and pierce the struggling companion whose hair is as long as its own.

Once the sacrifice is over, another stone in the necklace is touched: the arms drop, the smile and the eyes fall shut, and the murderess once again becomes the Maiden, motionless in its coffin.

II. Death by Water

He is standing. And he is standing as absolutely and definitely as if he were sitting.
WITOLD GOMBROWICZ

The road is covered in snow and, inside the coach, the somber lady wrapped in furs is bored. Suddenly she calls out the name of one of the girls in her train. The girl is brought to her; the Countess frantically bites her and sticks needles in her flesh. Afterwards, the procession tosses the wounded girl in the snow. The girl tries to run away. She is pursued, captured and pulled back into the coach. A little further along the road, they halt. The Countess has ordered cold water. Now the girl is naked, standing in the snow. Night has fallen. A circle of torches surrounds her, held out by impassive footmen. They pour water over her body and the water turns to ice. (The Countess observes this from inside the coach.) The girl attempts one last slight gesture, trying to move closer to the torches—the only source of warmth. More water is poured over her, and there she remains, forever standing upright, dead.

III. The Lethal Cage

...scarlet and black wounds burst upon the splendid flesh.

ARTHUR RIMBAUD

Lined with knives and adorned with sharp iron blades, it can hold one human body, and can be lifted by means of a pulley. The ceremony of the cage takes place in this manner:

Dorko the maid drags in by the hair a naked young girl, shuts her up in the cage and lifts it high into the air. The Lady of These Ruins appears, a sleepwalker in white. Slowly and silently, she sits upon a footstool placed beneath the contraption.

A red-hot poker in her hand, Dorko taunts the prisoner who, drawing back (and this is the ingenuity of the cage) stabs herself against the sharp irons while her blood falls upon the pale woman who dispassionately receives it, her eyes fixed on nothing, as in a daze. When the lady recovers from her trance and slowly leaves the room, there have been two transformations: her white dress is now red, and where a girl once stood a corpse now lies.

IV. Classical Torture

Unblemished fruit, untouched by worm
or frost, whose firm, polished skin
cries out to be bitten!

BAUDELAIRE

Except for a few baroque refinements—like the Iron Maiden, death by water, or the cage—the Countess restricted herself to a monotonously classic style of torture that can be summed up as follows:

Several tall, beautiful, strong girls were selected—their ages had to be between twelve and eighteen—and dragged into the torture chamber where, dressed in white upon her throne, the Countess awaited them. After binding their hands, the servants would whip the girls until the skin of their bodies ripped and they became a mass of swollen wounds; then, the servants would burn them with red-hot pokers, cut their fingers with scissors or shears, pierce their wounds, stab them with daggers (if the Countess grew tired of hearing the cries, their mouths would be sewn up; if one of the girls fainted too soon, she would be revived with burning paper soaked in oil between her legs). The blood spurted like fountains and the white dress of the nocturnal lady would turn red. So red, that she would have to go up to her room and change. (What was she thinking about during this brief intermission?) The walls and the ceiling of the chamber would also turn red.

Not always would the lady remain idle while the others busied themselves around her. Sometimes she would lend a hand, and then, impetuously, tear at the flesh—in the most sensitive places—with tiny silver pincers; or she would stick needles, cut the skin between the fingers, press red-hot spoons and irons against the soles of the feet, use the whip (once, during one of her excursions, she ordered her servants to hold up a girl who had just died and kept on whipping her even though she was dead); she also murdered several by means of icy water (using a method invented by Darvulia, the witch; it consisted of plunging a girl into freezing water and leaving her there overnight). Finally, when she was sick, she would have the girls brought to her bedside and she would bite them.

During her erotic seizures she would hurl blasphemous insults at her victims. Blasphemous insults and cries like the baying of a she-wolf were her means of expression as she stalked, in a passion, the gloomy rooms. But nothing was more ghastly than her laugh. (I recapitulate: the medieval castle, the torture chamber, the tender young girls, the old and horrible servants, the beautiful madwoman laughing in a wicked ecstasy provoked by the suffering of others.) Her last words, before letting herself fall into a final faint, would be: "More, ever more, harder, harder!"

Not always was the day innocent, the night guilty. During the morning or the afternoon, young seamstresses would bring dresses for the Countess, and this would lead to innumerable scenes of cruelty. Without exception, Dorko would find mistakes in the sewing and would select two or three guilty victims (at this point, the Countess's doleful eyes would glisten). The punishment of the seamstresses—and of the young maids in general—would vary. If the Countess happened to be in one of her rare good moods, Dorko would simply strip the victims who would continue to work, naked, under the Countess's eyes, in large rooms full of black cats. The girls bore this painless punishment in agonizing amazement, because they never believed it to be possible. Darkly, they must have felt terribly humiliated because their nakedness forced them into a kind of animal world, a feeling heightened by the fully clothed "human" presence of the Countess, watching them. This scene led me to think of Death—Death as in old allegories, as in the Dance of Death. To strip naked is a prerogative of Death; another is the incessant watching over the creatures it has dispossessed. But there is more: sexual climax forces us into death-like gestures and expressions (gasping and writhing as in agony, cries and moans of paroxysm). If the sexual act implies a sort of death, Erzebet Bathory needed the visible, elementary, coarse death, to succeed in dying that other phantom death we call orgasm. But, who is Death? A figure that harrows and wastes wherever and however it pleases. This is also a possible description of the Countess Bathory. Never did anyone wish so hard not to grow old; I mean, to die. That is why, perhaps, she acted and played the role of Death. Because, how can death possibly die?

Let us return to the seamstresses and the maids. If Erzebet woke up wrathful, she would not be satisfied with her tableaux vivants, but:

To the one who had stolen a coin she would repay with the same coin…red-hot, which the girl had to hold tight in her hand.

To the one who had talked during working hours, the Countess herself would sew her mouth shut, or otherwise would open her mouth and stretch it until the lips tore.

She also used the poker with which she would indiscriminately burn cheeks, breast, tongues….

When the punishments took place in Erzebet's chamber, at nighttime, it was necessary to spread large quantities of ashes around her bed, allowing the noble lady to cross, without difficulties, the vast pools of blood.

V. On the Strength of a Name

And cold madness wandered aimlessly
about the house.

MILOSZ

The name of Bathory—in the power of which Erzebet believed, as if it were an extraordinary talisman—was an illustrious one from the very early days of the Hungarian Empire. It was not by chance that the family coat-of-arms displayed the teeth of a wolf: the Bathory were cruel, fearless and lustful. The many marriages that took place between blood relations contributed, perhaps, to the hereditary aberrations and diseases: epilepsy, gout, lust. It is not at all unlikely that Erzebet herself was an epileptic; she seemed possessed by seizures as unexpected as her terrible migraines and pains in the eyes (which she conjured away by placing a wounded pigeon, still alive, on her forehead).

The Countess's family was not unworthy of its ancestral fame. Her uncle Istvan, for instance, was so utterly mad that he would mistake summer for winter, and would have himself drawn in a sleigh along the burning sands that were, in his mind, roads covered with snow. Or consider her cousin Gabor, whose incestuous passion was reciprocated by his sister's. But the most charming of all was the celebrated aunt Klara. She had four husbands (the first two perished by her hand) and died a melodramatic death. She was caught in the arms of a casual acquaintance by her lover, a Turkish Pasha; the intruder was roasted on a spit and aunt Klara was raped (if this verb may be used with respect to her) by the entire Turkish garrison. This however did not cause her death; on the contrary, her rapists—tired perhaps of having their way with her—finally had to stab her. She used to pick up her lovers along the Hungarian roads, and would not mind sprawling on a bed where she had previously slaughtered one of her female attendants.

By the time the Countess reached the age of forty, the Bathory had diminished or consumed themselves either through madness or through death. They became almost sensible, thereby losing the interest they had, until provoked in Erzebet.

VI. A Warrior Bridegroom

When the warrior took me in his arms
I felt the fire of pleasure…
THE ANGLO-SAXON ELEGY (8TH CENTURY)

In 1575, at the age of fifteen, Erzebet married Ferencz Nadasdy, a soldier of great courage. This simple soul never found out that the lady who inspired him with a certain love tinged by fear was, in fact, a monster. He would come to her in the brief respites between battles, drenched in horse-sweat and blood—the norms of hygiene had not yet been firmly established—and this would stir the emotions of the delicate Erzebet, always dressed in rich clothes and perfumed with costly scents.

One day, walking through the castle gardens, Nadasdy saw a naked girl tied to a tree. She was covered in honey: flies and ants crawled all over her, and she was sobbing. The Countess explained that the girl was purging the sin of having stolen some fruit. Nadasdy laughed candidly, as if she had told him a joke.

The soldier would not allow anyone to bother him with stories about his wife, stories of bites, needles, etc. A serious mistake: even as a newly-wed, during those crises whose formula was the Bathory's secret, Erzebet would prick her servants with long needles; and when felled by her terrible migraines and forced to lie in bed, she would gnaw their shoulders and chew on the bits of flesh she had been able to extract. As if by magic, the girls' shrieks would soothe her pain.

But all this is child's play—a young girl's play. During her husband's life she never committed murder.

VII. The Melancholy Mirror

Everything is mirror!
OCTAVIO PAZ

The Countess would spend her days in front of a large dark mirror; a famous mirror she had designed for herself. It was so comfortable that it even had supports on which to lean one's arms, so as to be able to stand for many hours in front of it without feeling tired. We can suppose that while believing she had designed a mirror, Erzebet had in fact designed the plans for her lair. And now we can understand why only the most grippingly sad music of her gypsy orchestra, or dangerous hunting parties, or the violent perfume of the magic herbs in the witch's hut or—above all—the cellars flooded with human blood could spark something resembling life in her perfect face. No one has more thirst for earth, for blood, and for ferocious sexuality than the creatures who inhabit cold mirrors. And on the subject of mirrors: the rumors concerning her alleged homosexuality were never confirmed. Was this allegation unconscious, or, on the contrary, did she accept it naturally, as simply another right to which she was entitled? Essentially, she lived deep within an exclusively female world. There were only women during her nights of crime. And a few details are obviously revealing: for instance, in the torture chamber, during the moments of greatest tension, she herself used to plunge a burning candle into the sex of her victim. There are also testimonies which speak of less solitary pleasures: one of the servants said during the trial that an aristocratic and mysterious lady dressed as a young man would visit the Countess. On one occasion, she saw them together, torturing a girl. But we do not know whether they shared any pleasures other than the sadistic ones.

More on the theme of the mirror: even though we are not concerned with *explaining* this sinister figure, it is necessary to dwell on the fact that she suffered from that sixteenth-century sickness: melancholia.

An unchangeable color rules over the melancholic: her dwelling is a space the color of mourning. Nothing happens in it. No one intrudes. It is a bare stage where the inert "I" is assisted by the "I" suffering from that inertia. The latter wishes to free the former, but all efforts fail, as Theseus would have failed had he been not only himself, but also the Minotaur; to kill the creature then, he would have had to kill himself. But there are fleeting remedies: sexual pleasures, for instance, can, for a brief moment, obliterate the silent gallery of echoes and mirrors that constitutes the melancholic soul. Even more: they can illuminate the funeral chamber and transform it into a sort of musical box with gaily-colored figurines that sing and dance deliciously. Afterwards, when the music winds down, the soul will return to immobility and silence. The music box is not a gratuitous comparison. Melancholia is, I believe, a musical problem: a dissonance, a change in rhythm. While on the *outside* everything happens with the vertiginous rhythm of a cataract, on the *inside* is the exhausted *adagio* of drops of water falling from time to tired time. For this reason the *outside*, seen from the melancholic *inside*, appears absurd and unreal, and constitutes "the farce we must all play." But for an instant—because of wild music, or a drug, or the sexual act carried to its climax—the very slow rhythm of the melancholic soul, not only rises to that of the outside world, it overtakes it with an ineffably blissful exorbitance, and the soul then thrills, animated by delirious new energies.

The melancholic soul sees Time as suspended before and after the fatally ephemeral violence. And yet the truth is that time is never suspended, but it grows as slowly as the fingernails of the dead. Between two silences or two deaths, the prodigious, brief moment of speed takes on the various forms of lust: from an innocent intoxication to sexual perversions and even murder.

I think of Erzebet Bathory and her nights whose rhythms are measured by the cries of adolescent girls. I see a portrait of the Countess: the somber and beautiful lady resembles the allegories of Melancholia represented in old engravings. I also recall that, in her time, a melancholic person was a person possessed by the Devil.

VIII. Black Magic

...who kills the sun in order to install
the reign of darkest night.

ANTONIN ARTAUD

Erzebet's greatest obsession had always been to keep old age at bay, at any cost. Her total devotion to the arts of black magic was aimed at preserving—intact for all eternity—the "sweet bird" of her youth. The magical herbs, the incantations, the amulets, even the blood baths had, in her eyes, a medicinal function: to immobilize her beauty in order to become, for ever and ever, *a dream of stone.* She always lived surrounded by talismans: In her years of crime, she had chosen one single talisman which contained an ancient and filthy parchment on which was written in special ink, a prayer for her own personal use. She carried it close to her heart, underneath her costly dresses, and in the midst of a celebration, she would touch it surreptitiously. I translate the prayer:

> *Help me, oh Isten; and you also, all-powerful cloud. Protect me, Erzebet, and grant me long life. Oh cloud, I am in danger. Send me ninety cats, for you are the supreme mistress of cats. Order them to assemble here from all their dwelling-places: from the mountains, from the waters, from the rivers, from the gutters and from the oceans. Tell them to come quickly and bite the heart of——— and also the heart of——— and of———. And to also bite and rip the heart of Megyery, the Red. And keep Erzebet from all evil.*

The blanks were to be filled in with the names of those whose hearts she wanted bitten.

In 1604, Erzebet became a widow and met Darvulia who was exactly like the woodland witch who frightens us in children's tales. Very old, irascible, always surrounded by black cats, Darvulia fully responded to Erzebet's fascination: within the

Countess's eyes, the witch found a new version of the evil powers buried in the poisons of the forest and in the coldness of the moon. Darvulia's black magic wrought itself in the Countess's black silence. The witch initiated her to even crueler games; she taught her to look upon death, and the meaning of looking upon death. She incited her to seek death and blood in a literal sense: that is, to love them for their own sake, without fear.

IX. Blood Baths

If you go bathing, Juanilla,
tell me to what baths you go.
CANCIONERO OF UPSALA

This rumor existed: since the arrival of Darvulia, the Countess, in order to preserve her comeliness, took baths of human blood. True: Darvulia, being a witch, believed in the invigorating powers of the "human fluid." She proclaimed the merits of young girls' blood—especially if they were virgins—to vanquish the demon of senility, and the Countess accepted the treatment as meekly as if it had been a salt bath. Therefore, in the torture chamber, Dorko applied herself to slicing veins and arteries; the blood was collected in pitchers and, when the victims were bled dry, Dorko would pour the red warm liquid over the body of the waiting Countess—ever so quiet, ever so white, ever so erect, ever so silent.

In spite of her unchangeable beauty, Time inflicted upon her some of the vulgar signs of its passing. Toward 1610, Darvulia mysteriously disappeared and Erzebet, almost fifty, complained to her new witch about the uselessness of the blood baths. In fact, more than complain, she threatened to kill her if she did not stop at once the encroaching and execrable signs of old age. The witch argued that Darvulia's method had not worked because plebeian blood had been used. She assured—or prophesied—that changing the color of the blood, using blue blood instead of red, would ensure the fast retreat of old age. Here began the hunt for the daughters of gentlemen. To attract them, Erzebet's minions would argue that the Lady of Csejthe, alone in her lonely castle, could not resign herself to her solitude. And how to banish solitude? Fill the dark halls with the young girls of good families who, in exchange for happy company, would receive lessons in fine manners and learn how to behave exquisitely in society. A fortnight later, of the twenty-five "pupils" who had hurried to become aristocrats, only two were left: one died some time later, bled white; the other managed to take her own life.

X. The Castle of Csejthe

The stone walk is paved with dark cries.
PIERRE-JEAN JOUVE

A castle of gray stones, few windows, square towers, underground mazes; a castle high upon a cliff, a hillside of dry windblown weeds, of woods full of white beasts in winter and dark beasts in summer; a castle that Erzebet Bathory loved for the doleful silence of its walls which muffled every cry.

The Countess's room, cold and badly lit by a lamp of jasmine oil, reeked of blood, and the cellars reeked of dead bodies. Had she wanted to, she could have carried out her work in broad daylight and murdered the girls under the sun but she was fascinated by the gloom of her dungeon. The gloom which so keenly matched her terrible eroticism of stone, snow and walls. She loved her maze-shaped dungeon, the archetypal hell of our fears; the viscous, insecure space where we are unprotected and can get lost.

What did she do with all of her days and nights, there, in the loneliness of Csejthe? Of her nights we know something. During the day, the Countess would not leave the side of her two old servants, two creatures escaped from a painting by Goya: the dirty, malodorous, incredibly ugly and perverse Dorko and Jo Ilona. They would try to amuse her with domestic tales to which she paid no attention, and yet she needed that continuous and abominable chatter. Another way of passing time was to contemplate her jewels, to look at herself in her famous mirror, to change her dresses fifteen times a day. Gifted with a great practical sense, she saw to it that the underground cellars were always well supplied; she also concerned herself with her daughters' futures—her daughters who always lived so far away from her; she administered her fortune with intelligence, and she occupied herself with all the little details that rule the profane order of our lives.

XI. Severe Measures

...the law, cold and aloof by its very nature, has no access to the passions that might justify the cruel act of murder.

SADE

For six years, the Countess murdered with impunity. During those years, there had been countless rumors about her. But the name of Bathory, not only illustrious but also diligently protected by the Hapsburgs, frightened her possible accusers.

Toward 1610, the king had in his hands the most sinister reports—together with proofs—concerning the Countess. After much hesitation he decided to act. He ordered the powerful Thurzo, Count Palatine, to investigate the tragic events at Csejthe and to punish the guilty parties.

At the head of a contingent of armed men, Thurzo arrived unannounced at the castle. In the cellar, cluttered with the remains of the previous night's bloody ceremony, he found a beautiful mangled corpse and two young girls who lay dying. But that was not all. He smelt the smell of the dead; he saw the walls splattered with blood; he saw the Iron Maiden, the cage, the instruments of torture, bowls of dried blood, the cells—and in one of them, a group of girls who were waiting their turn to die and who told him that after many days of fasting, they had been served roasted flesh that had once belonged to the bodies of their companions.

The Countess, without denying Thurzo's accusations, declared that these acts were all within her rights as a noble woman of ancient lineage. To which the Count Palatine replied: "Countess, I condemn you to life imprisonment within your castle walls."

Deep in his heart, Thurzo must have told himself that the Countess should be beheaded, but such an exemplary punishment would have been frowned upon, because it affected not only the Bathory family, but also the nobility in general. In the meantime, a notebook was found in the Countess's room, filled with the names and descriptions of her 610 victims, in her handwriting. The followers of Erzebet, when brought before the judge, confessed to unthinkable deeds, and perished on the stake.

Around her the prison grew. The doors and windows of her room were walled up; only a small opening was left in one of the walls to allow her to receive food. And when everything was ready, four gallows were erected on the four corners of the castle to indicate that within those walls lived a creature condemned to death.

In this way she lived for three years, almost wasting away with cold and hunger. She never showed the slightest sign of repentance. She never understood why she had been condemned. On August 21, 1614, a contemporary historian wrote: "She died at dawn, abandoned by everyone."

She was never afraid; she never trembled. And no compassion, no sympathy or admiration may be felt for her. Only a certain astonishment at the enormity of the horror, a fascination with a white dress that turns red, with the idea of total laceration, with the imagination of a silence starred with cries in which everything reflects unacceptable beauty.

Like Sade in his writings, and Gilles de Rais in his crimes, the Countess Bathory reached beyond all limits the uttermost pit of unfettered passions. She is yet another proof that the absolute freedom of the human creature is horrible.

Daria Dangerous

Shawn Dell

Daria was slick. I met her in a chic, midtown hotel bar. Actually, I didn't meet her. I was waiting there to meet a girlfriend. Daria was sitting alone at a table behind me, watching me. I set my motorcycle helmet on the chair across from me, where my girlfriend's sweet ass would soon be. I crossed my leather-covered legs, and tried hard to blend in with the stuffed shirts and ties. I could hear tittering under their breath… "Ooo, I'll bet *she* comes with whips and chains." Daria had a drink sent over to my table. She must have read my mind to know that I felt like a stiff gin and tonic, rather than my usual red wine. She was so smooth.

The woman who brought me the drink said her name, motioning to the dark woman in the suit who looked like she meant business, "Darrreeahhh." It rolled off her tongue like a sigh in the heat of passion—dripping wet, hot and half-moaned. Daria coolly eyed me over a tall crystal goblet. Dark eyes lined with black kohl, lips shimmering red. She looked delicious. She looked edible. I looked away, blushing. My friend walked up, as always slightly mortified by my antifashionable attire, slightly excited by the ruckus we caused. I couldn't control my eyes. I wanted to answer my friend's question, but my mouth could only form the word "Darrreeaahh." I was spellbound.

"What?" Michelle asked, following my gaze to the pale, dark enchantress who had me so speechless. Daria's eyes caught mine. Her eyes spoke to me. "Come here," they whispered, "Come to me." I got up and walked toward her. My girlfriend stared in disbelief at my barnyard manners. "Daarreeaahh," I breathed. Her eyes answered. I fumbled in my pocket to find a card, one of my artsy cards, and handed it to her. "Daria, I can't talk right now. I'm meeting a friend." Her eyes held my gaze, trapped me. I had the sensation of a giant magnet drawing me closer.

A slender hand with painted red nails swooped down on the card; the blood froze in my veins. She brushed my hand sending thousands of electrical sparks circulating through my body where once blood flowed freely. She examined the card, still not saying a word, and looked at me like a leading lady expecting the next line. "Thanks for the drink," I said, trying to break the trance. The whole bar was eavesdropping. I wanted so badly to appear normal, like I hadn't just flipped over this woman, winding up with a guest pass to never-never land.

Her lips parted and drew me toward them, beckoning as if each one had a tiny little voice, "Kiss me. Kiss me before you leave. Let me taste you." I bent to comply with my unspoken orders. I kissed her in what I had initially expected to be a polite peck, but my lips were glued to hers. We were causing a scene. I was on cloud nine and there wasn't even any tongue involved. Daria still hadn't spoken a word out loud to me, but her voice rang in my ears. It took all I could muster of what precious little control I seemed to have to pull away from this gorgeous denizen. I turned to face my incredulous friend and the gaping mouths of the other patrons. I felt like I was fighting the gravity of the moon as I pulled away. Daria's eyes burned holes through my leather jacket, boring through my flesh and into my heart where they leafed through the very essence of my soul, turning the pages flippantly, speed-reading my darkest desires.

"What the hell is wrong with you?" Michelle said, astonished.

"I, I don't know…that woman, Daarreeaahh. She bought me a drink. I went to thank her." Michelle peered around my back to the dark goddess.

"She looks strange." Michelle paused, "I get an eerie impression from her, like a ghost." I had known Michelle for ten years; we were close friends even though we lived on opposite sides of the continent. Normally, I would have trusted her inner voice as much as my own instinct. This time, I wanted to throw caution to the wind and not listen to her warning.

My own bells had gone off as well, but I had always been attracted to danger, and Daria's last name had to be Dangerous. The mysterious woman drained the red wine from her goblet and lilted a smile in my direction. I looked away to avoid staring, but my eyes were immediately drawn back to her: her table was empty. Ms. Dangerous had vanished. The exit was close enough that she could have run out, but she struck me as too cool to be in a hurry. No one else seemed to notice her absence. Slowly, as I began to regain control of my senses, I wondered if she were ever really there in the first place. A tall empty goblet glowed in the dim light, a trace of blood-red lipstick on its rim. She had been there. I tried to clear the fog from my brain as Michelle prattled on about her cats in San Francisco.

The New York City summer was rancid. Waves of heat rising off the pavement distorted the images of cabs careening down Fifth Avenue. I had taken a shower that morning, but felt like I hadn't dried off. The humidity plastered my hair to my skull and soaked through my clothing. My motorcycle was an inferno between my legs. I drove fast, darting in-between cars and just missing a collision with a semi-truck. I modeled my life after James Dean—I planned to live hard, die young, and leave a beautiful corpse. But not tonight. It was too fucking hot.

I sat on my little veranda and watched the burning sun dip into the horizon. All around me, the hum of air-conditioners drowned out the sound of the traffic. The sun had ruled the day with a riding crop, and as I toasted its dying embers, the dominatrix faded toward the other side of the world to beat it unmercifully with her heat. The sky overhead was bruised in the twilight. Purple clouds crisscrossed the pristine indigo like angry welts. My phone rang.

I couldn't find the energy to get up and answer it. I looked at the windows that were mocking me, distorting my reflection. A dark silhouette stood behind me on the terrace. I gasped, and turned. No one was there, but the phone was still ringing. Was this the tenth or the twentieth time? In slow motion, I got up and moved toward the beckon of the plastic device. "Yes," I said tersely (which was more polite than my usual greeting of, "Who died?").

"Good evening Sara. This is Daria. Am I disturbing you?"

The electric buzz in my head came back, clouding my rationality. *Oh yes, Daria, you disturb me—so deeply, so primally, so fucking erotically.* My mouth betrayed me: "Oh Daria, why no, I was just watching the sunset."

We made a date to meet in a nearby woman's bar, one I never went to. On my motorcycle, I buzzed through traffic like a hot knife through butter, slicing between the cars stuck at red lights, watching their grimacing jealous faces in my rear-view, and laughing my ass off. *Dyke on a bike, ride of your life, baby!* I cruised the West Village looking for the bar. I was late and she didn't seem like the type that one wanted to keep waiting. I had forgotten the pattern of one-way streets in the Village and was riding around the bar in wide circles trying to get close enough to park. *Bingo!* Found it, parked it, locked it. The night air wrapped around me like a girl-toy, hot and sweaty.

The bar was noisy and full. Gorgeous lesbians of all stripes eyed me as I strutted in. She sat in the darkest corner of the bar. I felt her eyes on me before I actually saw her. There were lots of eyes on me, but hers were different: exploring, looking up my shorts, toying with the rings in my nipples. She knew my body intimately before she ever laid a hand on it, save for a brush in the bar. She snagged my eyes in midair and held my glance. I moved through the crowd like a Christian on a mission from God. She drew me toward her, attracting me like so much shiny metal to a magnet. I was hot for her.

She looked beautiful: black clothes, lips lined and painted the brightest fuck-me red, half her 36Ds peeking at me, asking for a lick. I could drown in her eyes, smother in her tits, swim in her pussy. Her kohl blackened eyes appraised me. "You look lovely," she said.

My throat was trying to swallow my heart. I couldn't respond, so I smiled, and brushed her cheek with my lips, wanting to bite her flesh. I sat down beside her and she motioned to the bartender who immediately brought me a gin and tonic.

Damn! I thought, *How does she do that?* It was cool and wet on my throat, releasing the constriction.

Daria seemed to know the bartenders, and many of the women as well. Her glass was never empty; our ashtray never had more than two stubs in it before it was capped and replaced. Daria was sleek. Her dark, cropped hair was slicked back, little sideburns cut to sharp curls caressing her cheeks. In the dim bar, her skin was pallid, contrasting with her tight black chemise. We talked and made eyes at each other. A few sentences into our conversation, she leaned toward me; her lips parted invitingly. I didn't know whether she would bite me or kiss me, but I didn't care. I cocked my head forward to meet hers. Our lips melded; our tongues embracing, tasting, licking; our hands exploring, rubbing, fondling. We kissed for what seemed like an eternity. I forgot where I was, who I was, but not what I wanted.

One drink into the date, and I couldn't wait to go home with her. I asked her if she wanted to leave. She looked at me, and smiled. "I'll drive," she announced, taking my keys out of my hands before I could answer her.

The gin had gone to my head, but it was really Daria who had me so intoxicated. She picked up the extra helmet I had brought for her, pocketed my keys, and made for the door. I jumped up to follow her, unable to even form the question, *Can you drive a motorcycle?* I had never lent my shiny new toy to anyone, but Daria's self-confidence assuaged any doubts I might have had. She led me outside.

This girl always seemed to be one step ahead of me. She was unlocking the front fork lock and already had her helmet securely fastened. I wondered if she was as experienced in sex as well. She knew the ignition was by her knee. She turned the key and pressed the button that automatically started my iron horse, and my clitoris. She flipped up the kickstand with one deft movement of her leather-clad ankle, and gazing at me over her shoulder, purred, "Jump on, Baby!" I looked at her in amazement. She seemed to know my motorcycle *and* my body better than I did. "I used to hang with the Sirens when I was younger," she said as we pulled away from the curb with me riding bitch on my own bike.

I was familiar with the Sirens. They had surrounded me once at a stoplight, giving me the thrill of my young life. A group of leather Lost Girls looking for a nubile, they were all glossy and supernaturally beautiful. I had heard many stories about them tearing up bars and terrorizing seaside communities. It was also rumored that the Sirens were responsible for a number of unsolved murders in the area. Daria's admission gave me a new respect for her, born from fear. She seemed not to care about the effect her words were having on me. She drove smoothly down 14th Street, making every light. She was enchanting. I was falling in love.

Daria lived two blocks away from me, but it might as well have been another world. Her apartment was beautiful. A split-level with an incredible garden, two bedrooms, a real living room, and dining room. Several silky black cats caressed my ankles when I crossed the threshold. It took a moment for my eyes to adjust and soak in the scenery. She had decorated the place with antiques. Centuries old. Polished hardwood gleamed in the frail light. Then I noticed she had no windows—only velvet draperies covering the walls. Daria obviously had a great deal of money, and I felt painfully unworthy of her attention.

She fixed me another drink in a sprawling open kitchen. I thought of my own tiny apartment and the kitchenette I had built into my rough, unfinished loft. Drinks in hand, she glided gracefully across the floor. She motioned me to a room that contained only a bed in the center of it. The fabric that draped the shrine of bed glowed with white light and hung from ceiling to floor, but the bed itself did not touch the floor at all. It was suspended by chains from joists on the ceiling. She parted the transparent curtains, which smoothed over her automatically, obscuring her image in a haze of silk. As she sat on the edge of the bed, it rocked gently. Daria's eyes found mine, and for a second, I thought I saw a red glint light up the dark hollows. She patted a spot next to her in an invitation I couldn't refuse.

She laid me flat against the silver silk comforter. I felt her strong arms slide between mine and push them outward. Her long, slender fingers wrapped around my wrists and pinned them securely. Velvet cords seemed to appear of their own volition. She parted my legs with her own; her thigh slid between mine, insinuating itself warmly against my clit. Once again, I felt the velvet ropes, this time securing my ankles, her hands never leaving my wrists. I was bound to her magical bed. I surrendered to her completely without an ounce of resistance. She read my body like a dirty novel, skipping the plot, heading right to the sex scenes. She had a pipeline into my soul. We had no use for words; our bodies talked desire using a vocabulary of lustful sighs.

She reached under the corner of her bed and pulled out a satin blindfold. She stared deeply into my eyes, and although I had no idea who this witchy woman was, I allowed her to wrap it firmly over my eyes. I was totally and utterly at her dark mercy. Basking in her power and my abandon, she relished my vulnerability. I was in a trance. Her lips brutally smashed my lips against my teeth. I tasted blood. Her tongue probed deeply into my warm mouth. I was immediately hungry for more.

Some primal lust had woken inside me. I squirmed and bucked against the velvet restraints. Strange visions entered my head: dreams of flowers devouring each other, colorful beauties cruelly capturing each other in their kiss of death. I somehow knew this woman could kill me—and probably would—but the knowledge only made me want her more. Long nails raked my raw flesh. I could feel fire burst through my skin where her fingers traveled over it. Her nails combed through my pubic hair, spreading the heat. Her tongue traveled to my ear, snaked in and out and behind it.

She traced the line of my jaw with her mouth, all the way to my chin. She licked my neck with a raspy tongue as if she were tasting my flavor. Her mouth clamped around my throat, and she sucked. She held back her teeth, but I knew what she was, and what she wanted. As Daria worshipfully sucked, it all made perfect sense to me. Her pallor, the lack of windows, her ageless beauty, her heightened awareness—it all came together in a kaleidoscopic image of her dark side. I lost myself to her mouth. Arching my back, pussy throbbing, I knew I could come with Daria feeding on my neck. Then I felt her teeth. She sank them deep into the delicate flesh of my throat. Pain flared and ran coldly through the excited nerve endings of my body. Then I was quickly consumed by pleasure.

Funny things happen in the heat of passion: Time slows, bodies distort and fuse, unspeakable crimes occur. I questioned my sanity. How could I even imagine she was eating me? Sucking my blood? That was the last rational thought I had. Passion consumed my body, spurred by Daria, who read my thoughts and replaced them with her own. Heat mounted in my pussy, now gushing on the bed. My head exploded with fireworks. Bright colors lit up behind my eyelids. I had always known I would die at a lover's hands, but had never imagined it quite like that. I couldn't believe I was dying; I had never felt so alive!

Daria drank deep draughts of my life's blood, pulling it through her bloodstained lips, into her hungry mouth, and down into her supernatural body. I could hear the blood rush out of my body and into hers. We were one: predator and prey. I came hard, scraping my pussy raw against her thigh, lost in the light-headedness of sex and bloodlust. She drained me.

It took an amazingly long time for me to die. Daria wasn't satisfied with just my blood, she wanted my soul. She parted my legs, and pressed her bloodied and hungry mouth against my sex. I felt the teeth against my clit, scraping and pulling. She took my whole pussy into her mouth and fed on the juice. As she slowly killed me in the most pleasurable way, I could read her thoughts. Daria was draining my wiseblood, what Pagan women called menstrual blood, believing it held the secrets of the soul and the very essence of life. She was pulling me into the dark depths of her hell. I was her willing victim, a doe mesmerized by the headlights of a car.

My head swam in and out of consciousness as I came in Daria's mouth, giving her everything I had inside, pushing it down through my body and out into her gullet clamped over my womb. When she had taken it all, she cradled me in her arms. I had no regrets, no one who would miss me too badly. I felt strangely comforted by her embrace. My lover, my mother, my killer. All that was me was now inside Daria: my memories, my desires, my soul, my essence mingled with hers.

I did not fight the dark embrace of death. She held me as my bloodless body quivered and stilled, the life drained out. She held my dead corpse until dawn, rocking gently on her bed, singing my life's song into my lifeless, unhearing ears. My blue lips, wrapped around her warm red nipple, frozen in the first, and last, act of life.

Bibliography

Dynamo House. *The Angel Decoder.* Dynamo House Pty. Ltd. Melbourne, Australia. No date.

George, Demetra. *Mysteries of the Dark Moon: The Healing Power of the Dark Goddess.* Harper Collins, New York. 1992.

Guiley, Rosemary Ellen. *The Complete Vampire Companion: Legend and Lore of the Living Dead.* Macmillan, New York. 1994.

Keesey, Pam. "Introduction." *Daughters of Darkness.* Cleis Press, Pittsburgh. 1993.

Marigny, Jean. *Vampires: Restless Creatures of the Night.* Harry N. Abrams, New York. 1994.

Melton, J. Gordon. *The Vampire Book: The Encyclopedia of the Undead.* Visible Ink, Detroit. 1994.

Patai, Raphael. *The Hebrew Goddess.* KTAV Publishing House, Inc. New York, NY. 1967.

Salmonson, Jessica Amanda. *The Encyclopedia of Amazons: Women Warriors from Antiquity to the Modern Era.* Paragon House, NY. 1991.

Schwartz, Howard. *Lilith's Cave: Jewish Tales of the Supernatural.* Harper & Row. New York. 1988.

Walker, Barbara G. *The Woman's Encyclopedia of Myths and Secrets.* Harper Collins, New York. 1983.

About the Authors

Gary Bowen is a left-handed gay writer of Welsh-Apache descent from Waco, Texas, now living in exile on the East coast. In 1995, Masquerade Books published *Diary of a Vampire*, his erotic horror novel, which will be followed in 1996 by *Man Hungry: The Erotic Imagination of Gary Bowen*, a collection of erotic short stories in various genres. His other collections include *Queer Destinies*, gay science fiction (Circlet Press, 1994), and *Winter of the Soul*, gay vampire fiction (Obelesk Books, 1995).

Renee M. Charles lives in a houseful of cats, has a B.A. in English and also teaches writing. She has had over one hundred stories, poems and articles published in over fifty genre magazines and anthologies, including *Weird Tales*, *Twilight Zone* and *2 AM*.

Cora Linn Daniels was a member of the Society of Arya Samaj of Arya-Wart; Fellow of the Society of Science, Literature and Art, London; Fellow of the Royal Asiatic Society, London; and member of the American Folklore Society. Her novels include *The Bronze Buddha* and *As It Goes By*.

Shawn Dell is an emerging lesbian-feminist erotic writer and artist whose main stomping ground is Manhattan. She is frequently spotted touring on Medusa, her vampyre motorcycle, in search of adventure, material and her next victim.

Amelia G's work has appeared in publications ranging from *Chic* to *White Wolf* and she has been interviewed for various print and television specials on vampires. She edits *Blue Blood*, a magazine of counterculture erotica which includes lots of vampire sensuality. Amelia can be reached c/o *Blue Blood*, 3 Calabar Court, Gaithersburg, MD 20877-1036.

Carol Leonard is a certified midwife in practice for the last twenty years. She is the co-author of *Women's Wheel of Life* (Viking Penguin, 1995). She is currently on temporary sabbatical to conduct exhaustive personal research on the indigenous practices of vampires around the world.

Alejandra Pizarnik was born in Argentina, the child of immigrant Jewish parents. She published eight books of poetry before her suicide in 1972. Among them are *La tierra mas ajena* (1955), *La ultima inocencia* (1956), *Los trabajos y las noches* (1965), *Extraccion de la piedras de la locura* (1968), and *Nombres y figuras* (1969).

Thomas S. Roche is a writer and editor living in San Francisco. His short stories have appeared in *Black Sheets* and *Marion Zimmer Bradley's Fantasy Magazine.* Upcoming appearances include stories in the anthologies *Sexmagic 2* (Circlet Press), *No Other Tribute* (Masquerade Books), and *Truth Until Paradox* (White Wolf). He is currently editing an anthology of darkerotic mystery/crime stories for Masquerade Books.

Lawrence Schimel is twenty-three years old, lives in Manhattan, and works part-time in a children's bookstore. Schimel's stories have appeared in over fifty anthologies, including *100 Vicious Little Vampire Stories* and *The Random House Treasury of Light Verse.* His work has also appeared in *The Saturday Evening Post, Modern Short Stories, The Writer* and *Physics Today.* With Carol Queen, he is editing *Switch Hitters: Lesbians Write Gay Male Erotica and Gay Men Write Lesbian Erotica.* (Cleis Press, 1996).

Cecilia Tan is the publisher and editor of Circlet Press, specializing in erotic science fiction. Her work has appeared in *Penthouse, Paramour, Herotica 3* and *4, Sensual Delights: An Asian American Erotic Feast, By Her Subdued* and *Looking for Mr. Preston.* Running her own company gives her the freedom to sleep all day and work all night.

Melanie Tem is the author of *Prodigal, Daddy's Side, Blood Moon* and *Wilding,* in addition to collaborations with her husband, Steve Rasnic Tem. *Revenant* (Dell Abyss, 1994) is Tem's latest solo novel. *Making Love* (Dell Abyss, 1993), first in a "demon lover" series written in collaboration with Nancy Holder, will be followed by *Witch-Light* in 1995. *Desmodus* will also be published by Dell in 1995.

About the Editor

Pam Keesey is a writer, editor and book reviewer currently living in Minneapolis. She is the editor of *Daughters of Darkness: Lesbian Vampire Stories* (Cleis Press, 1993). Her future projects include two new books: *Vamps: An Illustrated Guide to Women as Vampires*, which explores vampire imagery from the ancient goddesses, the literary femme fatales and the vamps of the 1920s, to movie vampires and contemporary vamps such as Sharon Stone; and *Women Who Run with Werewolves*, a collection of short stories.

Books from Cleis Press

Sexual Politics

Forbidden Passages: Writings Banned in Canada introductions by Pat Califia and Janine Fuller.
ISBN: 1-57344-020-5 24.95 cloth;
ISBN: 1-57344-019-1 14.95 paper.

Good Sex: Real Stories from Real People, second edition, by Julia Hutton.
ISBN: 1-57344-001-9 29.95 cloth;
ISBN: 1-57344-000-0 14.95 paper.

The Good Vibrations Guide to Sex: How to Have Safe, Fun Sex in the '90s by Cathy Winks and Anne Semans.
ISBN: 0-939416-83-2 29.95 cloth;
ISBN: 0-939416-84-0 16.95 paper.

I Am My Own Woman: The Outlaw Life of Charlotte von Mahlsdorf translated by Jean Hollander.
ISBN: 1-57344-011-6 24.95 cloth;
ISBN: 1-57344-010-8 12.95 paper.

Madonnarama: Essays on Sex and Popular Culture edited by Lisa Frank and Paul Smith.
ISBN: 0-939416-72-7 24.95 cloth;
ISBN: 0-939416-71-9 9.95 paper.

Public Sex: The Culture of Radical Sex by Pat Califia.
ISBN: 0-939416-88-3 29.95 cloth;
ISBN: 0-939416-89-1 12.95 paper.

Sex Work: Writings by Women in the Sex Industry edited by Frédérique Delacoste and Priscilla Alexander.
ISBN: 0-939416-10-7 24.95 cloth;
ISBN: 0-939416-11-5 16.95 paper.

Susie Bright's Sexual Reality: A Virtual Sex World Reader by Susie Bright.
ISBN: 0-939416-58-1 24.95 cloth;
ISBN: 0-939416-59-X 9.95 paper.

Susie Bright's Sexwise by Susie Bright.
ISBN: 1-57344-003-5 24.95 cloth;
ISBN: 1-57344-002-7 10.95 paper.

Susie Sexpert's Lesbian Sex World by Susie Bright.
ISBN: 0-939416-34-4 24.95 cloth;
ISBN: 0-939416-35-2 9.95 paper.

Fiction

Another Love by Erzsébet Galgóczi.
ISBN: 0-939416-52-2 24.95 cloth;
ISBN: 0-939416-51-4 8.95 paper.

Cosmopolis: Urban Stories by Women edited by Ines Rieder.
ISBN: 0-939416-36-0 24.95 cloth;
ISBN: 0-939416-37-9 9.95 paper.

Dirty Weekend: A Novel of Revenge by Helen Zahavi.
ISBN: 0-939416-85-9 10.95 paper.

A Forbidden Passion by Cristina Peri Rossi.
ISBN: 0-939416-64-0 24.95 cloth;
ISBN: 0-939416-68-9 9.95 paper.

Half a Revolution: Contemporary Fiction by Russian Women edited and translated by Masha Gessen.
ISBN: 1-57344-007-8 $29.95 cloth;
ISBN: 1-57344-006-X $12.95 paper.

In the Garden of Dead Cars by Sybil Claiborne.
ISBN: 0-939416-65-4 24.95 cloth;
ISBN: 0-939416-66-2 9.95 paper.

Night Train To Mother by Ronit Lentin.
ISBN: 0-939416-29-8 24.95 cloth;
ISBN: 0-939416-28-X 9.95 paper.

Only Lawyers Dancing by Jan McKemmish.
ISBN: 0-939416-70-0 24.95 cloth;
ISBN: 0-939416-69-7 9.95 paper.

The Wall by Marlen Haushofer.
ISBN: 0-939416-53-0 24.95 cloth;
ISBN: 0-939416-54-9 paper.

We Came All The Way from Cuba So You Could Dress Like This?: *Stories* by Achy Obejas.
ISBN: 0-939416-92-1 24.95 cloth;
ISBN: 0-939416-93-X 10.95 paper.

Lesbian Studies

Boomer: Railroad Memoirs by Linda Niemann.
ISBN: 0-939416-55-7 12.95 paper.

The Case of the Good-For-Nothing Girlfriend by Mabel Maney.
ISBN: 0-939416-90-5 24.95 cloth;
ISBN: 0-939416-91-3 10.95 paper.

The Case of the Not-So-Nice Nurse by Mabel Maney.
ISBN: 0-939416-75-1 24.95 cloth;
ISBN: 0-939416-76-X 9.95 paper.

Dagger: On Butch Women edited by Roxxie, Lily Burana, Linnea Due.
ISBN: 0-939416-81-6 29.95 cloth;
ISBN: 0-939416-82-4 14.95 paper.

Dark Angels: Lesbian Vampire Stories edited by Pam Keesey.
ISBN: 1-57344-015-9 24.95 cloth;
ISBN: 1-7344-014-0 10.95 paper.

Daughters of Darkness: Lesbian Vampire Stories edited by Pam Keesey.
ISBN: 0-939416-77-8 24.95 cloth;
ISBN: 0-939416-78-6 12.95 paper.

Different Daughters: A Book by Mothers of Lesbians edited by Louise Rafkin.
ISBN: 0-939416-12-3 21.95 cloth;
ISBN: 0-939416-13-1 9.95 paper.

Different Mothers: Sons & Daughters of Lesbians Talk About Their Lives edited by Louise Rafkin.
ISBN: 0-939416-40-9 24.95 cloth;
ISBN: 0-939416-41-7 9.95 paper.

Dyke Strippers: Lesbian Cartoonists A to Z edited by Roz Warren.
ISBN: 1-57344-009-4 29.95 cloth;
ISBN: 1-57344-008-6 16.95 paper.

Girlfriend Number One: Lesbian Life in the 90s edited by Robin Stevens.
ISBN: 0-939416-79-4 29.95 cloth;
ISBN: 0-939416-8 12.95 paper.

Hothead Paisan: Homicidal Lesbian Terrorist by Diane DiMassa.
ISBN: 0-939416-73-5 14.95 paper.

A Lesbian Love Advisor by Celeste West.
ISBN: 0-939416-27-1 24.95 cloth;
ISBN: 0-939416-26-3 9.95 paper.

Long Way Home: The Odyssey of a Lesbian Mother and Her Children by Jeanne Jullion.
ISBN: 0-939416-05-0 8.95 paper.

More Serious Pleasure: Lesbian Erotic Stories and Poetry edited by the Sheba Collective.
ISBN: 0-939416-48-4 24.95 cloth;
ISBN: 0-939416-47-6 9.95 paper.

Nancy Clue and the Hardly Boys in ***A Ghost in the Closet*** by Mabel Maney.
ISBN: 1-57344-013-2 24.95 cloth;
ISBN: 1-57344-012-4 10.95 paper.

The Night Audrey's Vibrator Spoke: A Stonewall Riots Collection by Andrea Natalie.
ISBN: 0-939416-64-6 8.95 paper.

Queer and Pleasant Danger: Writing Out My Life by Louise Rafkin.
ISBN: 0-939416-60-3 24.95 cloth;
ISBN: 0-939416-61-1 9.95 paper.

Revenge of Hothead Paisan: Homicidal Lesbian Terrorist by Diane DiMassa.
ISBN: 1-57344-016-7 16.95 paper.

Rubyfruit Mountain: A Stonewall Riots Collection by Andrea Natalie.
ISBN: 0-939416-74-3 9.95 paper.

Serious Pleasure: Lesbian Erotic Stories and Poetry edited by the Sheba Collective.
ISBN: 0-939416-46-8 24.95 cloth;
ISBN: 0-939416-45-X 9.95 paper.

Reference

Putting Out: The Essential Publishing Resource Guide For Gay and Lesbian Writers, third edition, by Edisol W. Dotson.
ISBN: 0-939416-86-7 29.95 cloth;
ISBN: 0-939416-87-5 12.95 paper.

Politics of Health

The Absence of the Dead Is Their Way of Appearing by Mary Winfrey Trautmann.
ISBN: 0-939416-04-2 8.95 paper.

Don't: A Woman's Word by Elly Danica.
ISBN: 0-939416-23-9 21.95 cloth;
ISBN: 0-939416-22-0 8.95 paper

1 in 3: Women with Cancer Confront an Epidemic edited by Judith Brady.
ISBN: 0-939416-50-6 24.95 cloth;
ISBN: 0-939416-49-2 10.95 paper.

Voices in the Night: Women Speaking About Incest edited by Toni A. H. McNaron and Yarrow Morgan.
ISBN: 0-939416-02-6 9.95 paper.

With the Power of Each Breath: A Disabled Women's Anthology edited by Susan Browne, Debra Connors and Nanci Stern.
ISBN: 0-939416-09-3 24.95 cloth;
ISBN: 0-939416-06-9 10.95 paper.

Woman-Centered Pregnancy and Birth by the Federation of Feminist Women's Health Centers.
ISBN: 0-939416-03-4 11.95 paper.

Autobiography, Biography, Letters

Peggy Deery: An Irish Family at War by Nell McCafferty.
ISBN: 0-939416-38-7 24.95 cloth;
ISBN: 0-939416-39-5 9.95 paper.

The Shape of Red: Insider/Outsider Reflections by Ruth Hubbard and Margaret Randall.
ISBN: 0-939416-19-0 24.95 cloth;
ISBN: 0-939416-18-2 9.95 paper.

Women & Honor: Some Notes on Lying by Adrienne Rich.
ISBN: 0-939416-44-1 3.95 paper.

Latin America

Beyond the Border: A New Age in Latin American Women's Fiction edited by Nora Erro-Peralta and Caridad Silva-Núñez.
ISBN: 0-939416-42-5 24.95 cloth;
ISBN: 0-939416-43-3 12.95 paper.

The Little School: Tales of Disappearance and Survival in Argentina by Alicia Partnoy.
ISBN: 0-939416-08-5 21.95 cloth;
ISBN: 0-939416-07-7 9.95 paper.

Revenge of the Apple by Alicia Partnoy.
ISBN: 0-939416-62-X 24.95 cloth;
ISBN: 0-939416-63-8 8.95 paper.

You Can't Drown the Fire: Latin American Women Writing in Exile edited by Alicia Partnoy.
ISBN: 0-939416-16-6 24.95 cloth;
ISBN: 0-939416-17-4 9.95 paper.

Ordering Information

We welcome your order and will ship your books as quickly as possible. Individual orders must be prepaid (U.S. dollars only). Please add 15% shipping. Pennsylvania residents add 6% sales tax. Mail orders to:

Cleis Press
P.O. Box 8933
Pittsburgh PA 15221.

MasterCard and Visa orders: include account number, expiration date, and signature. Fax your credit card order to (412) 937-1567, or telephone Monday–Friday, 9 am–5 pm EST at (412) 937-1555.